TRUE VERT

To Olivia,
Enjoy!

TRUE VERT

A novel

Janet Eoff Berend

Janet Eoff Berend

BREAKAWAY BOOKS
HALCOTTSVILLE, NEW YORK
2016

ISBN: 978-1-62124-024-2
Library of Congress Control Number: 2016946769

Published by Breakaway Books
P.O. Box 24
Halcottsville, NY 12438
www.breakawaybooks.com

FIRST PRINTING

CONTENTS

OPPOSITE ENDS OF
THE SAME SITUATION

I used to be scared of Lenny. Like deer-in-the-headlights scared. But now Lenny's sitting behind a long table at the front of the courtroom in a suit that doesn't fit right. The jacket's huge, like he's swimming in it, he's practically being strangled by a blue tie clenched around his neck, and he sits, shoulders slumped, staring at the floor. Now, when I look over and see the bailiff dude standing at the front of the room, arms folded across his chest, a gun resting at his side, Lenny doesn't seem so scary anymore.

My name is called. My mom looks at me and smiles. A dab of lipstick is smeared across her front tooth and she keeps squirming around in her chair, like she can't find a comfortable way to sit. My dad reaches over, squeezes her hand, and then he locks his eyes on mine. *This is it*, I think to myself.

I head toward the witness stand and take a seat right under this huge picture of an eagle flying over an American flag, the words GREEN VALLEY SUPERIOR COURT, STATE OF CALIFORNIA written in big block letters underneath it. Studying me, the judge clears his throat. Then it's just like the lawyer said it would be. I state my name for the court. "Josh Lowman." My age. "Fifteen." The bailiff squeaks over, I take the oath, and the lawyer starts asking questions, lots of questions. So I repeat the same story I've already told a thousand times.

It was me, Brendon, Junior, and Lenny in front of Danny Ramsey's garage. It was dark, but not so dark that I couldn't see. Junior held me down while Lenny punched me. I tried my hardest to get away while Brendon just stood there. Brendon didn't punch *or* hold me, but he didn't try to help me either. And then Lenny freaked out, started swinging a skateboard around like the blade of a helicopter, came at me, heaving the board over his head like a giant heavy metal ax, bringing it down on me like I was a piece of dried-up wood he was trying to split in half.

"Tell the court, Josh," I hear the lawyer say, his voice filtering through the noise in my brain like light seeping through curtains. "Are you sure it was Lenny Fisher who hit you over the head with a skateboard? Are you absolutely sure?" Passing my hand across the back of my head, I feel the indented spots on my skull, run my fingers along scar tissue where doctors drilled holes to relieve the pressure on my swollen blob of a brain. Permanent reminders. The lawyer looks at me and nods. I stare at my shoes for a second. Then I look out at all the people in the room waiting for me to say something.

All I can think about is the heat. It's hot up here. Like hot as Satan's balls hot, and I keep hoping that someone will burp or fart or crack a joke, something, anything to create a distraction so I can disappear, but no one does and all I really want to do is loosen the tie cinched around my neck and go home because *everyone* in the courtroom, my mom and dad, my older sister, Hannah, my friends Erin, Niko, and Cody, Brendon and his mom, the judge, the lawyers, even the *bailiff*, stares at me, their eyes fixed on me like the viewing scope of a high-powered rifle.

I have to say something. I *know* I have to say something. So I sit there like an idiot searching for the right words. What I want to say is that even though I know that Lenny totally sucks for what he did to me and that he *totally* deserves to go to jail, there's this weird part of me that feels kind of sorry for him too. Especially when I see him sitting there—no family, no friends, no nothing—in that suit that doesn't fit right. Everyone is motionless, waiting to hear me talk, except Lenny who's shifting around in his seat staring at the ugly green tiles that cover the floor, looking exactly the way *I* feel, like he wishes he could curl up into a ball and disappear. And for a second I think about how me and him are on opposite ends of the same situation.

Trying to clear my head, I reach for a glass of water sitting on a little table next to me, when I notice Brendon fidgeting around in his seat too. He darts his eyes in my direction and then refocuses on the ground. Brendon. We met in the fifth grade. We spent a lot of time together . . . learned to skate together. I guess you could say he was pretty much my best friend, kind of like my brother. That was before the "untils." Like, *until* he started hanging out with Lenny. Or, *until* he stood there and watched Junior hold me down. Or, *until* he watched Lenny pummel me. And the best one of them all . . . *until* he left me in a dark driveway in a pool of blood and ran off with both of them. If it weren't for Erin, the girl who saved my life, I'd be dead right now. *Dead.* And all I ever wanted to do was be his friend and skate.

I let out a sigh. Everybody's eyeballs are still glued to me like

I'm about to reveal the secrets of the universe. The lawyer, impatient, jaw clenched, hands shoved deep into his pockets, clears his throat and rephrases the question, talking real slow. "Can you point to the person who beat you over the head with a skateboard?"

I take another deep breath and study the faces staring back my way one last time. I think about that night. I think about Lenny and Junior. I think about waking up in a hospital bed and not knowing where I was. But mostly I think about Brendon, the old one, and the new one. And then I point. "It was Lenny Fisher."

CALCULATED RISKS

The last bell of the day wails across campus. I stand up, stretch my body that's been crammed into a too-small school desk for most of the day, grab my board that's tucked in the corner of the classroom, and dip out the door. A mob of students rush into the parking lot. I bust through packs of kids standing around, high-five a few friends here and there, check to see that no teachers or vice principals are looking, and then I drop my skateboard on the pavement and bail.

On my way out of school, I pass by mine and Brendon's old weekend skate spot. I stop, stand there studying the terrain, and for a split second it's like Brendon's here, like the way it used to be—Brendon Johnson floating over the stairs, suspended in the air, his board flipping underneath him, he catches it with his feet like he has magnets in the bottom of his shoes, lands like magic, and for a second I forget about the judge reading the verdict, the bailiff leading Lenny and Junior out of the courtroom off to jail, Brendon and his mom never even looking over in my direction, standing up as fast as they can, and leaving as my lawyer leans over smiling, telling me we won the case. And then poof—four years of spending every minute of my life with Brendon, *four years* of epic skate sessions evaporate into the atmosphere and I'm left standing at the bottom of our old skate spot not really sure what happened.

I stick around staring at the empty set of stairs long enough that I'm one of the last kids left at school until I hop on my board, push myself along the concrete sidewalk, and cruise along the streets leading to the Green Valley Skatepark. When I finally get to the entrance, Cody's sitting on his board, his tall gangly legs like a grasshopper's, waiting for me in the shade. When he sees me, he pops up, a goofy grin spread across his face and long strands of red hair hiding half of his eyes. We high-five and then head into the park. A skater drops into the sweet, kidney-shaped nine-foot pool, grinds across the lip, his wheels click-clacking across the buttery tiles before he swooshes across smooth concrete, carves a turn, and pops out on the same side where he started. Skaters hoot and holler. But not Cody. His eyes are fixed on the vert ramp.

The top of the vert ramp juts out of the park and into the sky like one of those Mayan temples you see in world history books. You can see it from about anywhere in our flat town. It's two stories high and really long, like a giant, slithering 120-foot half-pipe serpent waiting to feed on its prey. It's so big that when you stand on the top platform and look toward the foothills, you see cars crawling around the roads in the distance like tiny ants. You're up *so* high that you're eye-level with the tops of trees. And when you stand at the edge and look into the bottom . . . it's sketchy. I'm talking drop-in-your-stomach, heart-in-your-mouth, adrenaline-pumping-through-your-body sketchy.

"You ready?" I ask Cody.

He looks down at his feet and nods.

We hop on our boards and roll over to the base of the vert ramp. We climb the stairs and when we get to the top, I rotate around in a 360-degree circle taking in the view while Cody stands at the edge contemplating the drop, totally silent.

"You got this, dude," I say. "No problem."

Looking toward the stairs, he takes a deep breath and then spins his gaze back toward me. "You go first," he mumbles.

I look him square in the eye and then drop my board to the ground. The sweet chunky sound of wheels smacking against the wooden platform rings and fades. I slide my board over to the coping, press on the tail with one foot to keep it there, and swivel my head back to look at Cody. His jaw is tight and he's shifting his weight from one foot to the other. He swipes a strand of red hair from his forehead and then moves his finger back and forth across the pattern of freckles splattered across his face. "Look," I say. "You just gotta decide you're gonna do it, that's all. Lean forward, bend your knees, and commit. You can pull this. I know you can. You just gotta *commit*."

He peers over the rail, eyes fixed on the concrete below.

"Dude, watch me. Just watch. It's not as big of a deal as you think." I stomp on the front of my board and drop in. I hurtle down the first wall, pump through the base of the ramp, shoot up the second wall, and blast into the sky. My back hand reaches around my knees, pegging my board to my feet, and with my other hand stretched out in front of me I soar through the sky like a cannonball. I pivot my body, arc through the atmosphere, and for an instant I'm weightless, floating, and then the clunking sound of my wheels echoes through the park and I reenter the ramp. I race down the second wall and fly up the first. Popping out the top, I catch my board in my hand and plant my feet on the platform right next to Cody.

"See, it's not that big of a deal," I tell him.

He looks at me and shakes his head. "Dude, I'm gonna go skate the street course," he says and bolts down the stairs.

I clomp down the stairs after him. When I finally catch my breath I see Cody standing by the water fountain next to the entrance. I skate up alongside him and take a long pull of water. I pop my helmet off and wipe drops of water from my mouth with my arm. I look at him, he looks at me, neither of us saying anything for a couple of seconds. Then Cody starts picking at the corner of some ratty old sticker that's halfway stuck to his helmet.

"You ever heard of calculated risk?" he asks.

I nod.

He spins a wheel on his skateboard. "We were talking about it in history class today, where you look at your chance to succeed, and compare it against your chance of failing. Like those bomber pilots in World War Two." He stops talking for a second and glances toward the vert ramp. It's quiet, and then he mumbles something real low under his breath so I can barely hear him: "It's just so sketchy."

In the distance, the vert ramp towers above everything else. A skater stands on the top platform, studying the drop. "Yeah . . . ," I say. "It is."

"So then if you're scared, *really scared*, how do you get that voice out of your head that tells you, you can't do it?"

I look at him. He looks at me. I chew on my bottom lip, not sure what to say, but I know exactly what he's talking about. *The voice.* Dropping in on the vert ramp the first time. Standing up there *forever*. Looking down the face. Wanting to drop in so bad for so long I could taste it. And Lenny and the trial and being so scared and so freaked out and so nervous that sometimes I couldn't sleep at night. And that voice, lingering in my head, telling me I didn't have guts, telling me I couldn't do it. Cody stares at me waiting for me to answer. "Sometimes you just have to take a calculated risk," I whisper, half speaking to myself and half answering Cody's question.

He nods. Then we both plop our boards on the ground and skate over to the street course. We skate the rest of the afternoon, sliding across rails and riding mini ramps until the sun dips behind the foothills. We pop off our helmets, slide off our pads, and join the mob of rabid skaters crowding around the snack shack counter. Skeeter, his scrawny ponytail resting along the back of his faded staff jacket, the waist of his pants sagging practically to his knees, stands behind the entrance window talking to some guy none of us recognize. Pretty soon some little kid hollers, "What the heck—I'm dying of thirst here." And the rest of us chime in, "Yeah, come on, Skeeter," "We're thirsty," "Do your job."

The guy Skeeter's talking to hands him a thick stack of papers and bails. Skeeter turns around to face us. Spitting a nasty wad of pink gum into the trash can, he wipes the corner of his mouth with his sleeve. "Shut your traps. Don't you know who that was?" he hollers. He looks at us and then, shaking his head, answers his own question. "That was Dirk Davies, you idiots—owner of ADSK. You know? *The* ADSK—Alpha Dog Skate Kru." He wags a finger at some kid who has a big ADSK logo on the front of his baggy T-shirt. "Dirk Davies is gonna come here and put on an insane skate contest, and all you morons can do is stand around and whine like little babies. You call yourself skaters? You ought to be ashamed." Letting out a high-pitched cackle, he hands out flyers to the pack of skaters who surround him like a bunch of starving wolverines. And then it's like a giant mosh pit. Arms and elbows fly everywhere. Skaters grab flyers like Skeeter's handing out Willy Wonka golden tickets. All me and Cody want is a cold drink and some Red Vines and we both know that's not gonna happen anytime soon. We grab a flyer, throw our backpacks over our shoulders, and head for the exit of the skate park.

Cody reads the flyer and then stops walking. Standing there, his skateboard dangling from one hand, he holds the ADSK paper in the air with the other. "Dude, you're gonna enter this thing, right?" The streetlights flicker on in the parking lot. I think about it for a second and then slowly, I shake my head no.

"Well, you should. You'd win."

He's smiling from ear to ear, his eyes all wide and lit up, and he starts talking as fast as he can, words spewing out of his oversized math brain. "Come on, Lowman. You *gotta* do it. It says right here, they're looking for new talent. Whoever takes first place in the vert competition has a shot at a spot on the ADSK team—that'd be rad." He shakes his head back and forth, grinning. "An ADSK team rider . . . Getting paid, dude. *Getting paid to skate.* Your picture in magazines. You kiddin' me? You're the best vert skater around. You *gotta* go for it."

I study a blade of grass poking out of a crack in the pavement, trying to picture myself skating in that contest, and when I think about a giant mob of people standing around watching, their eyes zeroed in on me as I drop in, all I can think about is falling. All the sudden, my stomach feels so queasy I feel like I'm gonna hurl.

I look up, blink a few times. Cody's staring at me like he knows. Like he can see the hairs standing up on the back of my neck. Like he can feel my stomach churning. He grabs me by the arm and starts talking in this super-low bullfrog voice. "See, sometimes, you just gotta commit," he says, "Sometimes, you just gotta take the risk." He laughs, tosses his skateboard on the pavement, and hops on. "See ya tomorrow, Lowman," he says and skates off.

I watch Cody get smaller and smaller as he glides away on his skateboard, disappearing around a corner. I look at the flyer in my hand. For a second, I think about wadding it into a ball and tossing it in the green-barrel garbage can next to the fence, but I fold it up and slide it into my back pocket instead. I hop on my skateboard and start pushing toward home.

I cruise along the sidewalk just outside the skate park, and right when I'm about to fly through a crosswalk I hear the deep, low rumble of a car engine. I stop just in time. A black car skids to a stop at the corner, cool rims spinning backward, a bright-blue racing stripe hugging the raised hood. I make eye contact with the driver to make sure he doesn't step on the gas and pummel me and when I look into the car I recognize the face. It's that Dirk Davies dude. His hand lies on the top of the steering wheel; his other arm rests along the shoulders of a pretty girl in the passenger seat of his ridiculously sick car. He looks up for a second, sees me, and gives me a nod. I cruise across the intersection, bust an ollie onto the sidewalk, and stop. I turn around just in time to see Dirk Davies roll around the corner. Revving the engine a few times, he tears down the street, his red running lights slowly fading into the purple night sky.

3

JERKS AND PHONIES

After math class I stroll through the quad looking for Erin. I spot her where we always meet up leaning against the wall outside the cafeteria talking to some guy I've never seen before. She twirls a strand of shiny brown hair around her finger and he stands there, his notebook resting in his hand, dangling at his side. He says something, she laughs, and then he turns around and walks away. She sees me and waves me over.

I walk across the quad toward Erin, my eyes glued to the vanishing frame of the dude who was talking to her. "Who's that poser?" I say, flicking my head in his direction.

"Matthew Cuttahy, he's in my science class."

"Looks like a poser."

"Just because he doesn't wear rags, he's a poser?" She grins, pointing to the hole in the knee of my favorite jeans. She plants her green eyes right on me. "He's okay. We're working on a project together," she says, heaving her backpack onto her shoulder and scooping up half a dozen books sitting on the ground. We start walking. Smiling, she bumps into me. I grab the stack of books out of her hands and then stick out my foot trying to trip her as we head to the library to work on our homework.

We find a table not too far away from the library lady, who looks at us smiling as we pass by. We put our stuff down. I put my backpack on the floor and drag out the book we just finished reading in my tenth-grade English class, *The Catcher in the Rye*. I toss it on the table in front of me. Erin digs around in her backpack for a pen and then looks up. She sees the book, picks it up, and runs her hand over the cover like she's touching hands with a long-lost friend. "Holden Caulfield . . . what a great book," she says.

My eyebrows scrunch together and I feel like maybe it's time to clean out my ears because I can't believe anyone could actually like *The Catcher in the Rye*—hands down the crappiest book I've ever read. "*Really?*" I say. "You liked *him? Holden Caulfield?*"

She shrugs. "I don't know, I kinda feel sorry for him," she says, shaking her head.

I sit there trying to figure out how Erin Campbell, the coolest girl I know, could actually *like* Holden Caulfield. I mean, whenever she says something about a book, I don't argue 'cause she reads *a lot* of books. But feeling sorry for a guy like Holden Caulfield? It's too much. "*Sorry for him?*" I say. "He's got it made. He's in New York City without parents on his back *and* he's got a wad of money in his pocket."

"Yeah, but he's all alone." She brushes a strand of hair behind her ear and sighs. "I mean, think about it. He doesn't have *any* friends. There's not *one* person who he can really talk to."

I lean forward in my chair. "That's 'cause he's a total whiner. And the worst part is, he's just like the people he whines about. *He's* the biggest jerk and phony in the book."

The library lady glances over at us. Erin twirls her hair, thinking.

Then she leans over toward me. "Because he's *mixed up*," she whispers.

"*Why?*" I ask.

"I don't know. I mean, he's not perfect. And you're right, he does complain a lot. He's a total mess, but at least he's *real* about it. You know what I mean? That's why I like him."

I nod, chewing the end of my pencil. I stare at the carpet under my feet for a second, then look up and meet Erin's gaze. "Well, can't he be not perfect and mixed up and real—all the stuff you're talking about—without being a jerk?" I say. "That's all I'm asking for."

Erin shakes her head. "You're impossible." Reaching over, she pinches my cheek like she's my grandma or something. I kick her under the table, she kicks me back and then she grabs my wrists and we both start wrestling around, books and papers flying everywhere. And when she puts her hands on me, when she wraps her fingers around my forearms and tries as hard as she can to pin my arms to the table, I make her think that I'm fighting as hard as I can, but I let her win. We crack up. The library lady, her eagle eyes homing in on us, asks us to keep it down. So we stop messing around and get down to business.

Erin grabs a pen and paper and helps me come up with an outline for the essay I have to write. Even though she makes it seem like writing an essay is super easy, I sit there, spinning my pencil, trying to figure out how to start. I guess I could write about what it's like to be mixed up, what it feels like to try to hold on to something that feels like it's slipping away—all the smart stuff that Erin talks about—but I decide to write something else. I write about how if Holden Caulfield doesn't like jerks and phonies he should stop acting like one.

I'm halfway done with the second paragraph when Erin taps me on the shoulder. "I gotta go," she says. I look at my watch and then around the room. We're the only ones left even though the library stays open for another half hour. I shove my stuff into my backpack and leave with her. We get to the curb just outside the school and Erin stops. "What are you doing?" I say.

"Waiting here."

"We're not gonna walk home like always?"

"Not today."

"Get a slushie or something?"

"Matthew Cuttahy's giving me a ride. We've gotta work on our project."

"Oh," I say and look down at my shoes.

"We can get a slushie tomorrow," she says.

"He drives?"

"Who?"

"Matthew Cuttahy. He's gonna give you a ride?"

"Well, yeah . . . he has a car," she says.

Then Matthew Cuttahy pulls up to the curb and Erin hops in the front seat. She hangs her head out the window. "See you tomorrow," she says, and they drive off just like that.

I stand there, not really sure what just happened. I look around. I'm alone except for the library lady, who's scurrying across the empty parking lot to get to her car. I hold my hand up to the fall sky and measure the amount of daylight left. Even though the days are getting shorter, the sun is more than a thumb away from the horizon, which means if I hurry, I can get home in time to skate in front of my house with Niko and Cody, but for some reason I don't feel like skating anymore.

When I get home I head straight to my bedroom. I dump my backpack on my bed and sit at my desk. The flyer for the ADSK Skate Jam hangs by a tack from the corner of my bulletin board. Just looking at it makes my heart start to beat a little bit faster, but I take it down and read it again anyway: *Take first place in the vert competition and you could become the next ADSK team rider.*

Tapping my fingers on my desk, I stare at the flyer in front of me and then I notice the envelope from the Department of Motor Vehicles that's tacked to my bulletin board too. I look over at the calendar hanging on my wall and count squares until I land on the box two months away when I turn sixteen and finally get my driver's license . . . a driver's license and no money and *no car.* I exhale long and loud. I get ready to finish my homework, but I can't focus because Cody's bullfrog voice and the words *getting paid to skate* keep swimming around in my head. I think about Dirk Davies with his arm around that girl in his passenger seat. But mostly I think about Erin . . . in Matthew Cuttahy's car. I grab the Skate Jam entry form, pick up a pen, and start filling it out.

4

DOG-EAT-DOG COMPETITION

Blue shade canopies fill the entire parking lot of the skate park. Giant speakers blast music, and Skeeter, wearing one of those red, green, and yellow beanies with fake dreadlocks hanging down the back, dances around a barbecue grilling up burgers and dogs. A guy standing next to a poster advertising Godzilla sports drinks hands out cans from a trash can full of ice and a huge banner hangs from the vert ramp, ALPHA DOGS SKATE JAM written across the front in giant letters next to a drawing of a gnarly pit bull in a studded collar, a slobbery skateboard dangling from its mouth.

I cruise through the mayhem searching for Niko and Cody. I spot Niko out of the corner of my eye. A backward ball cap sits on his giant head, skinny jeans cling to his legs, thick as tree trunks, and his favorite ninja warrior T-shirt hangs from his wide frame. Cody stands next to him looking like some kind of freckle-faced scarecrow. I walk up to them and give them high fives. We head over to a booth to check out all the skateboard decks with classic graphics and the posters of pros pulling insane tricks.

Eventually the three of us weave through mobs of people and finally reach the competitors' tent. Niko and Cody stand on each side of me and watch me sign up for the vert competition. We hear a deep voice boom from the loudspeakers announcing that the Skate Jam's going to start soon, so we make our way through the street course when someone taps me on my shoulder. I turn around. My math tutor, Zander, a toothpick teetering between his teeth, black-framed sunglasses clinging to his face, gives me a high five and then fist-bumps Cody and Niko. We squeeze through the throngs of people, stopping when we find a vacant spot under the vert ramp.

Zander stares at my number. "Big competition," he says, bobbing his head up and down. "You got your board set up right?" He plucks the toothpick from between his teeth and twirls it between his fingers. Nodding, I look down at my board, trying to play it cool.

Zander crouches down on one knee like a quarterback. Sliding his sunglasses to the top of his head, he looks up into our faces. "I used to skate contests all the time. There's a secret to how it works, you know?" We lean in closer. "It's pretty simple," he says. "Show up. Stick around. That's the secret."

Me, Cody, and Niko look at each other with blank stares, trying to figure out Zander's Yoda-speak. Shaking his head, Zander laughs. "Look. Here's the deal. A bunch of dudes are gonna go really big, bust out tricks they can't land. They're gonna fall and lose points. Then there'll be the cats who are too conservative because they don't want to fall. Boring *and* low scoring. Here's what you're gonna do. You're gonna show up, skate, and stick around long enough to let those other guys lose."

"But you still gotta skate good enough to win," Niko blurts out.

"Yeah. You gotta show up and skate. But the difference between you and the other guys is, you're gonna use *strategy*." Zander flicks his head toward Cody. "How many tricks can Josh land?"

Before Cody can say anything, Niko jabs Cody in the arm and answers for him. "Are you kidding me? He's a maniac. He can land all kinds of sick tricks."

Zander looks at me. "Okay, so . . . take five of your best tricks that you *know* you can land and spread 'em around the ramp. Simple math."

"He's right," Cody says, rubbing the spot on his arm where Niko pegged him, wagging his head up and down like he's just discovered new life-forms on Mars. "You can. You can use math to your advantage."

Niko reaches toward Cody, getting ready to finger-flick him in the ear. "Lighten up on the nerd factor, would ya, Alice."

Cody swats his hand away like it's some kind of annoying bug and then cocks his arm back ready to smack Niko upside the head. "I told you. Don't call me Alice." Hooting and laughing, Niko leaps behind me, taking cover. I step to the side, exposing Niko to the heinous death wrath of Cody, aka Alice, agitated scarecrow, math nerd out for revenge.

When Zander stands up, I think my face is turning green. My stomach is doing flips and I feel like I'm gonna either hurl or crap my pants. Zander looks at me. "Josh," he says, "you've been practicing your runs, right?" I nod. "So close your eyes and picture yourself skating the vert ramp, like you're watching a movie of yourself in your head. Watch yourself dropping in, choosing your line, setting up your tricks and landing 'em. Watch yourself do it over and over." He tosses me a bottle of water and I catch it right before it hits the ground. "Just go out there and skate . . . like you do all the time. That's all it is. It's just skating. You'll be fine." He pats me on the shoulder.

I find a place under the vert ramp and sit on my board. Closing my eyes, I do exactly what Zander tells me. I watch myself drop in. I stand on the top deck, stomp on the front of my board, and swoosh into the ramp over and over. I feel something brush against my shoulder and I think it's the wind, but then I hear someone say my name. When I open my eyes Erin's sitting across from me on the pavement holding her knees to her chest. "You ready?" she asks.

"Yeah." I swallow.

"You're a skater. This'll be easy, right?"

"Duh," I say, giving her a half smile.

"Take these." She hands me a stack of homemade oatmeal cookies wrapped in clear plastic. "I made them for you. They're for good luck."

"That's awesome," I say and set them down next to me.

Leaning over, she puts her hands on my knees. "Okay, I'm going to tell you everything I know about skate competitions." I nod, waiting for her to tell me. "Don't fall," she says. "And when you're done, we'll go get a slushie to celebrate." She smiles, her eyes dancing as we both stand up. She puts her hands on my shoulders. "Seriously. Don't worry. You're going to do great," she says, hugging me before she walks away, her brown hair swaying from side to side across her back, and then she turns around and waves to me before vanishing into the crowd. My stomach does another one of those flip things, but I'm not totally sure it's because I'm nervous about the contest. I reach down, grab my stuff, and race back to where Niko, Cody, and Zander are hanging out.

The announcer's voice booms over the skate park, "All vert

competitors, please check in at the vert ramp." We head to the bottom of the vert ramp stairs. A bunch of kids huddle there. I know a few from the skate park, but there's one kid standing in the middle of a bunch of skaters I don't recognize. Arms crossed against his chest, his foot rocks his board back and forth across the smooth pavement, and the strap to his helmet dangles underneath his chin. His buddy slaps him on the back. "Jagger, dude . . . you got this," he says. "You're gonna *kill* it!" Jagger pops the tail of his board against the ground and grabs it with his hand; he doesn't say a word, just stands there focused on the vert ramp.

Pretty soon a tall dude with stringy hair and a scraggly red beard shows up holding a clipboard in his hand. He rattles off the names of everyone competing in the vert ramp event and then goes over the rules. We all get three runs that'll last one minute. The judges rate each run and take our highest score. The top five skaters are placed in a semifinal and then the process starts all over again until there are two skaters left, who will duke it out in the final for the ADSK Top Dog title. He pops a sunflower seed into his mouth. Cracking it open with his teeth, he spits the empty shell into the breeze. "Any questions?" he asks.

Jagger spins a wheel on his board, then stops it with his finger. "How long?" he blurts out.

Red Beard pops another seed in his mouth. "How long what?"

"How long's it gonna take?"

Locking his eyes on Jagger, he stops chewing the seed. "As long as it takes," he says and then calls out each of us by our last names.

We line up. The skaters I know are in the front: Buddy Duran, this kid everyone calls Big Chad, and then me. That Jagger Michaels kid is right behind me and then there's a bunch of skaters

I've never seen before. We head up to the top platform of the vert ramp to start the first round. I watch the guys ahead of me skate. Buddy Duran busts really nice airs and he's pretty stylish too, but it's exactly like Zander said it would be. I can tell that Buddy doesn't want to fall so all he does are indy grabs and easy lip tricks and even though he looks good doing it, I don't think the judges are impressed. Big Chad keeps trying to bust these huge air tricks and he can't land anything, so toward the end of his run he winds up doing a couple of rail slides just to try and stay in the game.

Then it's my turn. I hear my name announced over the loudspeakers. The sound bounces off the walls and echoes through the park. A taste of metal creeps into my mouth, and beads of sweat bust out on my nose. I set my board up on the coping. I feel time stand still for a second, like everything's happening in slow motion. I take a deep breath, then the buzzer wails indicating my time has started. I stomp on the front of my board, start my run— and as soon as I start skating something really weird happens. I stop thinking and do what I do every day, just like Zander said . . . I skate.

I shoot down the first wall and come up smooth and in perfect position for my first trick. I hit the coping and fly out of the top of the ramp. Using all my forward momentum, I scoop the board up, bring my knees into my chest, tuck my body into a tight ball, and reach around my knees, grabbing the nose of my board all in one fast motion. I'm up in the air high, flying, rotating my body as fast as I can so I can spot the landing. I burst back into the ramp, my wheels smacking the surface as I reenter, blaze up the next wall, grind across the coping on my back truck, drop back in and set up for my next trick. Before I know it, the minute's up. I pop out of the ramp, plant my feet on the platform and grab my board with my hand.

It's totally silent for a split second, and then I hear the crowd explode. Buddy pats my back and Big Chad gives me a high five. The judges hold up their scorecards. I get the highest-scoring run so far and I think to myself, *I can do this . . . I'm gonna do this*, when Jagger Michaels walks past me, bumps into me hard, and I lose my balance. I'm teetering on the edge of the ramp about to plummet to the bottom, but Big Chad grabs my shirt and keeps me from falling. Jagger stops for a second, looks at me. "Be careful," he says and walks over to the drop-in spot. I'm ready to knock his lights out, but before I can do anything they announce his name over the loudspeaker.

Jagger, setting his board up on the lip, waits for the buzzer. As soon as his time starts, he zooms into the ramp. He starts off airing out of the top, grabbing his board with his back hand between his knees, and then he spends the rest of the time doing flip tricks on the coping, and he's good. He pops, spins, catches his board with his feet, gliding down the walls of the vert ramp like it's nothing. He makes it look easy, like anyone can drop in on the face of a fourteen-foot vertical wall with wheels under their feet, no problem. Landing every trick in his run, he pops out of the ramp right as the end buzzer rings.

He looks over at his crew, smirking. The judges hold up their scorecards and the cocky smile on his rat face fades because he scores two points *less* than me. He looks over at me. Turning his head, he spits off the edge of the ramp before heading toward the stairs. I take a step back so he can pass, but I don't take my eyes off him.

Big Chad manages to land some tricks on his third run. He makes it into the semifinal along with me, Jagger, and two kids who aren't from around here. Me and Big Chad head down the stairs of the vert ramp to get a cold drink before we skate again and when we get down to the bottom, Niko, Cody, Zander, and Erin surround us, slapping the backs of our helmets and giving us high fives. We pick our usual spot under the vert ramp, where I toss my board and helmet. Jagger and his crew hang out across the way, staring at us and talking to each other in low voices. Me and my friends walk right past them, heading over to the snack shack where Skeet's kicking back in the shade. As soon as he sees us, he pops up and slaps me on the back.

"Josh, my man," he says, giving me and Big Chad high fives. "You guys are dominating."

"Just having some fun." Big Chad plops his skateboard on the ground and plants a foot on it.

"That's what we like to hear at the lovely Green Valley Skate Eztraaavagaaaanza." Skeeter rubs his hands together then stretches his arms out, palms facing the sky. "Gentlemen . . . let me make you a burger," he says.

We all walk over to the Godzilla drink guy. He tosses us a bunch of cold cans to chug while we wait for our food. I can smell the burgers, finally relaxed enough that I'm actually starving, my stomach grumbling. We hustle back over to Skeeter. Pushing plates of food our way, he rests an elbow on the counter and leans in toward me and Big Chad. "Don't tell nobody, but these are on the house."

"Thanks," we say at the same time, and start laying into our food.

"Y'know, you two guys could take the whole enchilada here."

Skeeter points at us, wagging his finger back and forth. "You two make the final, we got two of our very own Green Valley boys taking first and second place. You know what that means, don't you?" Rocking back on his feet, he folds his arms across his chest. "Bragging rights." He looks around, reaches under the counter, and grabs something. "You gotta be well nourished if you're gonna get the job done." Sliding a couple of pieces of Red Vines our way, he lets out a cackle, flaps his arms like chicken wings, and dances over to his kick-back spot in the shade.

We hear the call for the start of the semifinal over the speaker. Big Chad grabs his board; we toss our plates in the trash can and hustle over to our spot under the vert ramp. I go to grab my stuff. My helmet sits there, but my skateboard is *gone*, disappeared, nowhere. I can't believe it. I look around from side to side, and then I remember the smarmy look on Jagger's face when he saw me set my board down. Dropping my face into my hands, I shake my head. "I can't believe it. I'm such an idiot," I mutter under my breath.

The gang comes over to where I'm standing. "Don't worry, Josh, we'll find it," I hear Erin say, and even though she's right next to me it sounds like she's a million miles away. Then everyone, Niko, Cody, Zander, Erin, and Big Chad, starts looking everywhere—under people's backpacks, in trash cans. I look around too, but in the pit of my stomach I know that we're not gonna find it—that I'm gonna be sitting on the sidelines watching Jagger take first place. We hear an announcement over the loudspeaker: "All semifinalists, report to the top deck." I let out a loud groan and everyone starts scurrying around like busy ants, giving one last desperate sweep hoping to find my stolen board until we realize it's a lost cause. My board is gone.

I plop down next to my helmet. I look at Big Chad. "Get up there. You're our only chance," I say.

He stands there looking at his skateboard for a few seconds, then picks it up and holds it out in my direction. "Here," he says. "Take it."

I focus on Big Chad's face towering above me.

"You're a better skater than me. Seriously. You actually have a chance at winning." He holds his board out, waiting for me to pluck it out of his hands.

I stand up and brush the dirt from the back of my jeans. I take a deep breath, study the board resting in Chad's hands, and then I look in his eyes and I know that's it over. I know that no matter what he says, he wants a shot at that spot on the ADSK team. Just like me. "No." I shake my head. Swallowing the lump in my throat, I slowly push Big Chad's board back toward him. "You got this," I say.

Zander puts a hand on my shoulder. Taking the board from Big Chad, he flips it over and spins one of the wheels. "You guys ride a board that almost has the same setup."

Big Chad locks his eyes on Zander and nods.

"Josh, it's a long shot riding a board you're not used to, but why don't you share?" Zander pushes the board toward both of us.

Erin, Cody, and Niko start talking at the same time. "Share the board, that's it," they babble like they're all singing the chorus to the same song.

I grab Big Chad's board and tic tac around the pavement. It feels different from what I'm used to riding, but I know if I'm gonna skate, I don't really have a choice. We hear the announcer call out "Chad Griffiths, Josh Lowman, get up to the top deck now or you're disqualified!" I pop the board up, hand it to Big Chad, and we both tear up the stairs to the vert ramp.

When we get to the top, Jagger's standing there. He looks surprised to see me. He looks at my empty hands, smirking. "Can't skate without a board, can you?" he says.

I look him right in the eyes. "Some piece of crap stole it."

"Yeah, well, it's dog-eat-dog in these competitions." He walks past me and heads to the corner of the platform to wait for his turn.

SUDDEN DEATH

Big Chad starts out his semifinal run solid, but then goes for a crazy flip trick and doesn't land it. A victim of the semifinal sudden-death, no-second-chances rule, he taps me on the shoulder and hands me his board. "Looks like I'm toast," he says. He fishes a skate tool out of his back pocket. "Tighten the trucks a little and you'll be fine." He brushes his hands together, then cruises over and leans against the rail to watch the action.

A couple of kids I don't know take their turns. They do all right, but I know if I have a good run, I can beat them. I flip Big Chad's board over in a panic. I don't have a ton of time so real quick I turn the bolts on the trucks a hair, turn the board over again, and test it out in place. It feels just about right. Then they call my name.

"Good luck," Jagger sneers from his corner. Shooting him a death stare, Big Chad comes off the railing, fists clenched and leading with his chest. He moves toward Jagger, ready to squish him like a bug. I hop in front of him. "It's cool," I say, "I got this." I take a deep breath and set Big Chad's board up against the coping. I close my eyes, think about my run, try to remember the order of tricks I planned, and try to forget that I'm on a board I've never ridden. Then the buzzer sounds and I shoot down the ramp.

Big Chad's board feels okay, but it's not what I'm used to. I try hard not to think about it, to stay focused, to just skate. I boost out of the ramp, scoop the board into my back hand, bring my knees to my chest so I'm in a nice tight ball. I use momentum and my shoulders to rotate my body and board around, and while I'm up in the air, I kind of straighten my front leg like I'm doing a karate kick before I spot the landing. But when I clomp back into the ramp, my board, or my feet, or something isn't right—like my body's going one way, and my board's going another. I drag my hand across the floor, my body leaning, and I'm hoping . . . praying, that this isn't it, that it's not over, that Jagger's not gonna win. Then with every muscle in my body, I hang on. Recovering, I stay on the board.

I can't remember what trick I had planned next 'cause I'm so rattled, but I know I gotta put together a decent run or I'm not gonna advance. I go with a simple trick, a rock to fakie, so I can clear my head. Then I race up the next wall, pop the tail and lock my back truck on the coping, pop the board up catching it with my feet, and do a half rotation in the air before rolling back in. I do a few more airs, getting some pretty good boost out of the ramp, but I don't try anything too fancy. I finish my run by sliding across the lip of the ramp backside, angling my way back into the ramp, and popping out the other side. I can't believe I survived the run without falling. I'm glad it's over.

The judges hold up their scorecards and I'm afraid to look, but when I turn to see the cards they're waving over their heads, my jaw drops. I score high enough to be in first place in the semifinals. The stands explode with hoots and hollers. I wave to the crowd, then look over at Jagger, bust out a full-on pearly white smile, and pump my fist in the air. He stares at me with his beady rat eyes, pushes past me, and heads over to the lip of the ramp. Big Chad gives me a high five and then wraps his arms around me in a big bear hug, lifting my feet off the ground. He puts me down and we settle back against the railing to watch Jagger skate.

Big Chad looks at me and I know we're both thinking the same thing. *Fall.* All we need is for Jagger to *fall.* If he falls, he's out—sudden death—no second chances—and we both know that's what he deserves. But he doesn't fall. He's unstoppable. He grinds, stalls, flips frontside and backside and he's smooth and powerful and in control. He goes for an air trick, boosts out of the ramp, uses his back hand to grab his board between his knees, and even though he's aggressive on the rail, technically skilled on the coping, his style turns to crap when he's in the air. His butt sticks out from bent knees, and like a giant smelly stinkbug he flies through the sky, lands the aerial, and gets back to his precise work on the lip of the ramp. He pops out of the ramp smiling, and even though his aerials are so ugly they make me want to puke, even I know he just put together a solid run.

He stands on the platform waiting for the judges to wave their cards over their heads, and when they finally do, Jagger has the highest-scoring run in the semifinal. Holding his board up in the air with one hand, he lets out a giant victory whoop. His hooligan friends hoot and holler and whistle. He slams his board down. Standing at the edge of the ramp, he beats his chest one arm at a time like King Kong and then he turns around, looks right at me, and smiles before he snatches his board up and bolts down the stairs. The announcer's voice booms across the entire skate park: "Ladies and gentlemen, please join us for the final heat of the

Alpha Dog Skate Jam between Joooooosh Lowman and Jaaaaaag-
ger Michaels! Show starts in ten minutos."

Big Chad puts his hand on my shoulder. "You gotta beat him,"
he says.

"I know," I whisper, and I can already feel my nerves wreaking
havoc in the pit of my stomach. I grab Big Chad's board and we
head down the ramp.

The first thing we do is head over to the mini ramp. I take a
few runs and stop in between to adjust the trucks on Big Chad's
board. I get the board totally dialed in so I have one less thing to
worry about. Then we meet up with the rest of the gang. Everyone
is super stoked, high-fiving and hugging me. I'm the only one not
having a good time because I know I have to go back up there and
skate. Zander pulls me away from the crowd. We find a semi-quiet
spot under the vert ramp and sit down. Zander fishes around in
his backpack and hands me a bottle of water. "You can beat this
guy," he says.

I take a sip of water and stare off in the distance.

"Seriously, you can. He's a street skater on a vert ramp. You're
a *vert skater* on a vert ramp."

I look at him, my head tilted to one side. Zander unscrews the
top to his water bottle. "He's good on the coping, I'm not gonna
deny him that, but this is *vert* skating and vert's all about air." He
takes a pull of water, then keeps talking. "You get *huge* air, Josh.
You're boosting three or four feet higher out of the ramp than
anyone in this contest. *And* you've got *great* style. What you need
to do is capitalize on that kid's weakness and cash in on your
strength."

I look at him with a blank stare. "You just gotta relax," he says, then fishes around in his backpack again and pulls out a pen and paper.

"What's that for?" I stare beyond the shadow of the vert ramp, then look at my watch.

"We need a plan," Zander grins. "Let's talk about your best tricks. You can pull a three sixty, of course." I nod. He starts scribbling. "How about a five forty?" I nod again. He looks up. "A seven twenty?" I clench my jaw, scrunch up my forehead. "Didn't think so—no problem." He taps his pen against the paper. "Rattle off the tricks you're most comfortable with." I talk, he writes, and even though I'm nervous, part of me is cracking up because Zander's like one of those mad scientists you see in cartoons, except instead of handling smoking beakers in a lab coat inventing the next atom bomb, he's formulating the perfect skateboard run. He kind of forgets I'm there for a second, writing stuff down, crossing it out, and mumbling to himself. Finally he looks up and smiles. "Got it," he says.

We go over the paper and it all makes perfect sense. The announcer calls us back to the vert ramp. "Remember, stay up in the air. Get as much air time as you can and you've got this joker beat."

I get to the top of the ramp and don't even look over at Jagger. I have Zander's paper in my hand and I study it, going over the tricks one by one in my head, concentrating, staying focused. I try to pretend that it's just me up there, just me and my board, and for the most part I feel pretty calm. The announcer calls my name, "Jooooosh Lowman." "You can do this Josh," I hear someone scream from the crowd. I recognize the voice—it's Erin. I take one last look over the railing before I get ready to skate, and I'm not sure, but I think I see *Brendon*. I can't *believe* it. I move to the railing to get a closer look, and I'm pretty sure it's him, but then Red Beard comes over and grabs my arm. "Showtime, buddy," he says and escorts me over to the drop-in spot.

I set my back trucks against the coping, focus on the drop, and wait for the buzzer. As soon as it sounds I plummet into the ramp. I pump through the bottom, getting tons of speed as I race up the opposing wall. I approach the coping, and my back foot's right in the pocket. I scoop the tail, boost into the air as high as I can, and I'm soaring. I turn my shoulders as hard as I can, whip them around, and get a full, sweet 360-degree rotation. I burst back into the ramp fakie, use the wall I started out on to set up my next trick, shoot back into the ramp, pump through the bottom for speed, and burst into the air again. I'm having so much fun skating that I'm actually surprised to hear the end buzzer ring. I pop out of the ramp and the crowd goes crazy. When the judges hold up their scorecards they erupt even louder.

Jagger stands against the rail clenching his jaw. I've forced his hand and he knows it. He's gonna have to spend less time on the lip and get up in the air if he's gonna beat me. I walk over to him. "Good luck," I say. He looks at my grinning face. "Screw you," he says and heads over to the edge of the ramp to get ready for his turn.

The buzzer sounds and Jagger drops in. He shows off on the lip for his first few tricks and his pop, flip, stall stuff is totally sick. I know that if he can pull some decent air tricks he's gonna be hard to beat. His first air trick goes smoothly and even though he doesn't boost as high out of the ramp as I do, he lands a 360. He's putting together a perfect run—the combination of lip tricks and airs, street and vert skating joined together as one—exactly what the judges like to see.

With only eleven seconds left on the clock, he goes for a stall on the coping. For an instant he's frozen in time hanging on the lip, and when he repositions his body to drop back into the ramp his back truck gets hung up on the edge. He's teetering, flapping his arms around in giant circles, trying to maintain his balance, trying desperately to dislodge the back wheel clinging to the coping like it's been bathed in superglue. And in an instant, in one glorious instant, he *falls*. Landing on his knees, he slides down into the pit of the ramp, shaking his head, swearing at the top of his lungs; loud curse words bounce off the walls and vaporize into the atmosphere. Sudden death. The crowd *explodes*.

I'm dazed, not really sure what just happened, but then Red Beard comes over, puts his hand on my shoulder, and says, "You won!" He guides me over to the railing so I'm facing the throngs of people below. Over the loudspeaker, the announcer's voice booms through the skate park: "Ladies and gentlemen, your Alpha Dog Vert Champion, Joooosh Loooooowman!" Red Beard juts my hand up into the air and the crowd goes absolutely nuts. They're chanting "Top Dog, Low-man, Top Dog Low-man."

I race down the ramp to Zander, Cody, Niko, Erin, and Big Chad. Lifting me up on their shoulders, they carry me through the skate park. People laugh, hoot, holler, and for a second I wonder if Brendon is in the crowd but then the gang sets me down and a photographer from the *Green Valley Times* newspaper pops out of nowhere and snaps our picture. Out of the mob, a man emerges. "Nice job up there," he says, pressing something into the palm of my hand. "We'll talk soon." Then he vanishes back into the chaos. I peek at the card—DIRK DAVIES, ALPHA DOG SKATE KRU,

OWNER/PRESIDENT. I glance in the direction of Jagger Michaels, who is pouting in a corner surrounded by his posse of jackass friends. They stole my board, the one Zander gave me when I was in the hospital. I know I'll never see it again, but I got what I came for. Smiling, I slide the card into my back pocket and reenter the mass of people chanting my name.

6

CONTRACTS

My dad sits at the kitchen counter drinking a cup of coffee next to a mountain of *Green Valley Times* newspapers. "What are those for?" I ask. He holds up the front page. There's a photo of me spinning a 360 in the air, blue sky and skinny clouds behind me, the lip of the vert ramp below with a caption in big, black letters: LOCAL SKATEBOARDER IS THE TOP DOG AT ALPHA DOG SKATE KRU COMPETITION. "Your mother made me go out and buy every copy I could find. She's going to send one to every relative east of the Pacific Ocean." My dad shakes his head, laughs to himself, and takes a sip of coffee.

I pour myself a bowl of cereal. Sitting next to my pop, I check out the newspaper when the phone rings. "For you," my dad says, handing it to me.

I hold the phone to my ear. "Hello, Josh?" A voice I don't recognize seeps through the line.

"Yeah?"

"This is Dirk Davies with Alpha Dog Skate Kru."

"Oh . . . Hi." Standing up, I push my cereal bowl to the center of the counter.

"Great job yesterday. You put on a heck of a show. I'd like to come by and talk to you sometime. Would that be all right?"

"Uh . . . yeah. Sure," I stammer.

"Good. How does five o'clock this evening sound?"

"Great. That'd be great."

"Perfect. And have your parents there. I'd like to meet them, too."

"No problem," I say and hang up the phone. I lean against the counter practically in shock.

"What's wrong?" my dad asks.

"Nothing . . . nothing's wrong," I say, a wave of excitement coursing through my blood. "You and Mom gonna be here later on, like around five?"

"Yeah. Why? What's up?"

"The owner of this super-rad skate company wants to talk to me."

"What for?"

"I don't know, Dad." I shrug. "It's an enigma." Smiling to myself, I sit back down and finish the rest of the soggy cereal floating in my bowl.

At exactly five o'clock the doorbell rings. I race to the door. Dirk Davies and some roly-poly dude with a briefcase stand there. Dirk shakes my hand. Sunglasses rest on top of his head, his slicked-back hair glistens in the evening light, and a breath mint teeters between two front teeth, perfectly white and gleaming. The guy standing next to him has a shiny bald dome of a head surrounded by a crown of brown curly hair. Brand-new skate shoes hug his feet, and a button-down shirt rests underneath an unzipped ALPHA DOG hoodie. His round belly is poking out from his shirt, his stumpy legs are being strangled by a pair of too-tight skinny jeans, and even though he's dressed like a skater I'm pretty sure he's never touched a skateboard in his life. He sticks out his hand. "Nice to meet you. The name's Artie," he snorts and gives me a quick handshake, too.

We stand around being polite and stuff, and then my parents escort us into the living room and we all sit down. Dirk doesn't waste a second. "At ADSK we're looking for young skaters with potential. We want to groom them . . . shape them, mold them into the next generation of ADSK talent," he says. Artie nods in agreement and my parents and me sit there listening quietly. Dirk goes on for a while talking about the dominance of his company—how he's looking to build a team of the hottest young skaters in the world, but I get kind of distracted because my seven-year-old brother, Mikey, is sitting at the top of the stairs making funny faces at me. I give him the evil eye and he scurries down the hall just in time for me to hear Dirk say, "We'd like Josh to train with us exclusively at our state-of-the-art training facility." Dirk leans forward in his chair and looks at each of us in the eyes. "What I'm saying, Josh . . . Mr. and Mrs. Lowman . . . is that we'd like to offer Josh a position on our team."

I can feel the blood coursing through every part of my body and I can hear my heart thumping in my ears. Artie pulls a piece of paper out of his briefcase, *a contract*, hands it to my parents, and I feel like everything is happening in slow motion. My mom and dad look at the paper, at each other, at me, and then the questions start.

"So what exactly does it mean that he's a team member?" "Will he have to miss school?" "Are there costs involved?" "Where's the training facility?" "What if he gets hurt?" I can hardly stand it. I'm ready to snatch the contract out of their hands and sign it before Dirk changes his mind, but Dirk, real calm, handles my parents like a pro.

"Here's how it works," he says. "Josh signs on as an ADSK team rider. We supply him with everything he needs to skate— clothes, equipment—*whatever he needs*. He trains and skates with us exclusively at our training facility, competes in skate competitions exclusively as one of our team riders, and . . . we pay him."

"I'd do all that for free," I pipe in, and everyone except me and Dirk laughs. Dirk looks at me real serious. "What we're looking for is a rider with tons of potential, someone we can develop into a big air machine. I see what you have to offer." He leans forward in his chair. "Become an ADSK rider . . . you're going to be cutting-edge."

Cutting-edge . . . the words ring out in my head. Artie hands my mom a pen and signals my parents and me to sign the contract. I'm so fired up, I can hardly sit still, but then my mom looks at my dad, and they both say the same thing at the same time: "Give us some time to think it over." Before I can open my mouth to try and talk some sense into my clueless parents, Dirk and Artie stand up and my mom and dad walk them to the door. "We'll be in touch," my dad says and they leave.

As soon as the door shuts I start in. "Are you *crazy*? What was that all about?"

My mom looks at me and shakes her head. "Sweetheart, you don't just sign a contract without looking it over," she says before heading into the kitchen.

"She's right. One hundred percent right. Life Lessons 101, son. Never sign a legally binding document until you've read it and thought it over," he says, putting his hands on my shoulders and guiding me into the kitchen.

I plop down on a stool at the counter. "I don't get it. I don't understand. What's there to think over?"

"Lots of things." My mom starts digging around in the refrigerator. "School . . ." She pops her head out of the fridge. "*Grades.*"

I shake my head. "Didn't you hear what Dirk said? I'm gonna get *paid* to skate. I'll make *money* . . . I'll buy my *own car.*"

My dad pulls some pasta out of the cupboard, puts a big pot under the faucet, and turns on the water. He leans against the sink. I hear the water running, and all I can think about is the ADSK contract slipping through my hands. "We're not saying no, Josh, we're just saying we want to talk it over before you make a commitment," my dad says. He turns the water off, puts the pot on the stove, and turns up the heat.

"What about that Dirk Davies guy? I don't like him," my mom says while she chops a carrot.

I take a deep breath and exhale. "Whaddya mean, Mom?"

"He's just so . . . polished. I don't know, there's something about him."

"So let me get this straight," I say, trying really hard not to lose it. "You're not gonna let me join the ADSK team because you think Dirk Davies is *polished?*"

My mom stops chopping. She looks at me right in the eyes. "No, that's not it."

"Then what is it, Mom? . . . *Please?*"

"It's just . . ." She blows out a sigh. "I don't want you to get *hurt*, that's all." She turns to my dad. "You heard Dirk. He wants to turn Josh into a *big air machine*. Have him do even scarier tricks than he's already doing. What if Josh gets hit in the head again?"

My mom turns back to face me. "I know this is important to you, but you have to remember, you had a *really* serious brain injury . . . I don't care what this Dirk Davies promises you, we need to think about this . . . *really* think about it."

My dad comes over from the stove and rubs my mom's shoulders. "You're right. Absolutely right. We need to think about this." I'm looking at him, begging, pleading with my eyes, and then he says, "But we also have to remember that Josh knows what he's doing on a skateboard."

I exhale. "I do, Mom. I do know what I'm doing. And I'd get paid . . . paid to skate. I'll save money, buy my own car. And I won't hit my head. I promise. I'll be careful."

My dad pops a piece of cut-up carrot into his mouth and tosses the rest into the salad bowl. "I think we should let him do it. Not every kid gets an opportunity like this. He'll learn a lot."

My mom stands there, a stack of plates in her hands, thinking. She sets the plates on the counter. "You need to bring your grade up in science or you're not going to pass the class."

It's quiet for a second. All I can hear is my heart pounding in my temples. Then my dad says, "Well . . . how 'bout this? Dirk has a contract with you. You have a contract with us?"

Me and my mom look at him.

"It's simple." My dad leans against the counter. "Josh, you have a contract with us—you get Zander to help you in science. You agree to stay focused on your schoolwork and help out around the house. You got the dishes tonight, no complaining. You wear your helmet at *all* times *with* the chin strap fastened. We'll get an attorney to take a look at Dirk's offer and if everything checks out, we sign the contract with ADSK." He looks at my mom. "What do you think, Ann?"

She stands frozen, altering her gaze from me to my father, and then finally, she slowly nods. "Okay," she says, shrugging.

I spring across the room and give them both a huge hug. "Awesome," I say, beaming.

Just then the pot on the stove boils over and my dad, spinning around, turns down the heat.

PHASE CHANGE

I stand at the window watching the first winter storm dump buckets of rain on the ramp in our backyard when my little brother comes over and drags me into the kitchen. He grabs a chair, climbs up on it, and pulls down a tattered cookbook from the top shelf in our cupboard. It's one that my mom used with me when I was a kid. I glance out the window and sigh. A pool of water forms in the middle of our backyard, and with the constant patter of rain against the roof it's gonna take days before it's dry enough to skate again. Mikey flips through the cookbook until he finds the sticky page he's looking for and then looks at me. He tilts his head. "Please?" he whines.

"Fine," I mutter and start dragging ingredients out of the cupboard.

When we're through, there's flour on the floor and dirty bowls in the sink, but there's also a pile of super-rad chocolate chip cookies that kind of look like hockey pucks, but taste delicious. After we stuff our faces, I take a plate and put some cookies on it. "What's that for?" Mikey asks, a streak of chocolate smeared across his face.

"Erin," I say, scribbling a quick note on a piece of paper. *Don't worry. These aren't turds.* I draw a big smiley face around the words.

After dinner me and my mom hop in her beat-up mini van. She sits shotgun and has me practice driving to the tutoring center so I can pass the gnarly driver's test that I'm going to have to take soon to get my license. We swing by Erin's house. We pull up. I park in her driveway, grab the cookies, hop out of the car, and ring the doorbell. She answers in sweatpants and bare feet. Ducking inside, I hand her the plate. She hugs me, tells me I'm sweet, and then walks into the kitchen, talking about her physics project. I follow behind but stop before I get there because I can't believe what I see. That poser Matthew Cuttahy is sitting at her kitchen table with all his books and papers and stuff spread out everywhere.

"Josh, this is Matthew," Erin says.

"Hey," I say.

He nods at me. "Hey," he answers, and then he keeps reading from some stupid thick science book.

Erin rambles on about school and soccer tryouts and her physics project, but I'm not really listening 'cause I'm too busy studying "Mr. Science Project Jackass" sitting at Erin's table. He has wide shoulders and a thick neck. He's wearing a crisp T-shirt and clean jeans, and his sneakers are practically sparkling they're so new. His hair is perfectly trimmed and kind of spiked up on his head. He looks . . . polished. Totally polished. I look down at my toe popping out of the hole in my sneaker and brush my mop of hair away from my eyes. Erin's standing in the kitchen munching on one of the cookies I made.

"Josh, these are *really* good!" she says. "Want one?"

"Nah, tutoring," I mumble.

"Matthew?" she asks, holding out the plate in his direction.

"Sure," Matthew says to Erin, stuffing his face with three of her cookies in rapid succession without even glancing at me.

I turn around to leave and Erin follows me to the door. "Thanks for the cookies. See you tomorrow," she says.

I bolt back to the car and as soon as I hop into the driver's seat, my mom fires off a round of questions: "What did she say? How'd she like them?"

"She liked 'em," I say, driving the rest of the way without saying a word.

When I get to Bright Horizons Learning Center, Zander's sitting at a table waiting for me. I dig an enormous textbook out of my backpack and set it on the table.

"Chemistry, my favorite," Zander says. He grabs the book and starts looking through it, "I *love* this stuff."

Typical Zander. He asks what chapter I'm on before laying the book on the table so we can both see it. "Chapter five," I say.

He flips the book open. "Phase Change. Simple stuff," he says.

I stare at a picture of a drop of water with a big black arrow pointing to an ice cube, then another picture of a drop of water with another arrow pointing to a pot of water on the stove with wavy blue lines that are supposed to be steam.

"So . . . What do you think the pictures are trying to tell you?" Zander asks.

"I dunno," I say, shrugging.

"Come on. Look at it. It's telling you something about water. What's it saying? I'll hook you up with some Skittles if you get it right."

"That water freezes and water boils?"

"Exactly. And what happens to water when it freezes or boils?" Zander leans his elbow on the table.

"It changes?"

He smacks the table with his hand. "Exactly—phase change! You got it!"

I look at him funny and he slides me a package of candy across the table.

"Okay, let me explain," he says. "Phase change is a fancy way of describing changes that occur when there's a change in the environment. So think about it. What happens if you put water on the sidewalk on a hot day in the middle of summer?"

"It evaporates," I say, popping a bright blue Skittle into my mouth.

"Yep! What happens to lake water high up in the mountains during winter?"

"It freezes?"

"Okay, so what conclusions can you make about water and temperature?"

"That water changes depending on what's happening outside?"

"That's it, Josh. That's all phase change is. Things change depending on what's happening in the environment. Water can be lots of different things. It's not always liquid. It can be solid or vapor too. So it changes back and forth, but molecularly speaking it's still water."

I nod. We read all the different charts about phase change. Zander explains what all the pictures and arrows and numbers mean and we eat so much candy that both of our mouths are blue by the time my tutoring session is over.

After working with Zander a couple more times, my grade in science is solid and finally, my parents let me go to the Alpha Dog training facility, forty-five minutes away, to start skating as an Alpha Dog team rider. The first day that I show up, Dirk's assistant, Charlie, meets me in the front office and shows me around. The facility is beyond rad—a skater's dream come true. A huge platform deck rests right up against the edge of a super-tall vert ramp. Me and Charlie climb two flights of stairs to get a closer look. Built into the platform deck is a giant pit shaped like a rectangle swimming pool, but instead of water the pool's filled with bright-colored chunks of foam. Right next to the foam pit and at the same level is a trampoline. "Air awareness training"—Charlie nods toward the trampoline—"and if you think this is cool, check that out." He points to the far end of the warehouse. "We have the best in-door street course in the USA. That baby over there is one-of-a-kind."

We climb down the stairs and head toward the street course when I hear a voice. Dirk Davies walks up to us. "Josh." He holds out his hand and we shake. "What do you think?"

"I think it's . . . *amazing*," I say, looking around.

"Glad you like it. We want you skating out here all the time— five days a week, Monday through Friday, rain or shine." Dirk turns to Charlie. "Take him over to the warehouse. Get him cleaned up. Replace his entire wardrobe. I want him in head-to-toe Alpha gear—a walking billboard. And do something about his hair." He makes his hand into a fist and runs it across his head. Dirk shakes my hand one more time then starts moving backward. "Have Steely get Josh started on vert today." He spins around and walks toward his office.

Charlie leads me down a hallway. We take a right turn, entering into a gigantic room filled with rows and rows of every Alpha Dog Skate Kru item I've ever seen. There are T-shirts, jeans, shoes, socks, ball caps, and hoodies everywhere. Charlie hands me some empty grocery bags, hops onto a table, and sits there. "Go for it," he says. I look at the grocery bags, then around the room, not really sure what I'm supposed to do. "You heard Dirk. ADSK head-to-toe." He hops off the table, starts grabbing stuff and handing it to me. When we're done I have three full bags of clothes, four new pairs of shoes, and a couple of ball caps.

Charlie heads for the door. "Stay here and change into some of your new clothes. I'll be right back," he says and ducks out of the room. I kick my tattered shoes off, get out of my old jeans, and slide into my new ADSK stuff. Charlie comes back into the room holding some funny-looking electric-razor thing in his hand. "Sit here," he says, tapping the seat of a fold-up aluminum chair before throwing a towel over my shoulders. He plugs the razor into the wall. I freeze as he starts shaving my head. When Charlie finally turns the razor off, mounds of hair sit at my feet. He sweeps it into a dustpan and dumps it in the trash. Brushing his hand across my scalp, he pops a ball cap on my head. "Go check it out," he says, gesturing toward a full-length mirror in the corner of the room.

I'm afraid to look, but I cruise over to look at myself and I can't believe what I see. Just like Dirk said, I'm a walking billboard—ADSK gear from head to toe. The only thing that doesn't have a logo on it are my boxers. Stepping closer to the mirror, I take off my ball cap and run my hand over my fuzzy head. I hardly recognize myself. My new haircut makes my eyes look bigger, my jaw looks kind of square, and in all my new clothes I look polished, but in a cool skater kind of way.

Charlie hands me my old clothes and my ratty shoes. I hold them in my arms in a wadded-up ball. "Follow me," he says. I think about stuffing my old clothes in one of the grocery bags with my new stuff, but I don't want to mix the old with the new. A mountain of my hair sits in the trash can. I decide that my old clothes belong there too. I throw them in the garbage can, grab the bags of new gear, and as I follow Charlie down the hall I check myself out in the windows that we pass. I can't believe that it's me that I see in the reflection.

Charlie leads me into the "board room." Brand-new ADSK skate decks rest against the walls, stacked one on top of the other until they're as high as my chest. A see-through glass counter with shelves—wheels, trucks, bearings, skate tools, and grip tape stacked in tidy rows—sits in the middle of the room. "You in here, Steely?" Charlie shouts. We hear some rustling around in the back office.

I walk around checking things out and I feel like I'm in some kind of sacred museum. Posters of old-school skating legends wearing headbands and tube socks that go up to their knees, blasting out of empty swimming pools on wide, stumpy boards, hang on the walls. There's one poster that stands out from the rest. The words DAVEY MCSTEEL, GODFATHER OF AIR are splashed across the top in big black letters and a super-cool photo sequence of this guy doing an insane trick bursts off the wall. In the first shot he's flying out of the deep end of an empty swimming pool. In the next he's in the air upside down, his skateboard pressed against his feet with big, neon-green wheels facing toward the sky, and in the final photo he lands back into the pool crouched down with his knees kind of pressed forward, his back hand grabbing the toe side of his board, his front arm stretched out in front of him like the wing of a gull.

Some totally ancient dude emerges from the back room. He's barrel-chested, and his big torso doesn't look like it should be attached to such skinny legs. Faded tattoos cover massive biceps, and piercing blue eyes gaze out from his leathery face. "Whatcha want, Charlie?" he rasps.

Charlie stretches his hand in my direction. "This is Josh Lowman, our new team rider. You're gonna be coaching him." He gestures toward the old man. "And Josh . . . this is Dave McSteel."

"*The* Davey McSteel?" I point to the poster on the wall without taking my eyes off the old man. "That Davey McSteel?"

He looks toward the poster, then back at me. "That was a long time ago . . . me in a different life," he grunts. "Don't even skate anymore." He turns around and moves toward the glass counter. He kind of rocks back and forth when he walks, like one leg is shorter than the other, and even though he kinda limps it doesn't slow him down. He moves like he's a general in the army or something. He slides the door to the glass counter open, then looks me up and down. "You a vert skater, right?" he asks.

I nod.

He reaches into the glass case. "You pull a five forty?"

"Yeah," I say, "but I don't land 'em every time."

"Hmmm." He starts pulling wheels and trucks out and sets them on the counter. "Grab a couple skate decks you like from the pile there." He gestures with his head.

Charlie and me start sorting through the decks until I find a couple I like. We hand them to Mr. McSteel and he starts putting them together. He pops trucks on the decks and tightens the bolts without even looking at his hands. I think he could put together a skateboard in his sleep. He stops what he's doing for a second, waves a gnarled finger in my direction. "You," he says, "grab some knee pads and a helmet for that fuzzy coconut of yours." He taps his finger on his head. "And you, Charlie, grab a deck from the pile there," he orders. When he's through he hands me a board, then grabs the second board from the counter and tosses this strange-looking skate deck to Charlie. It has these foot-strap binding things bolted to the top of it and no wheels or trucks attached to the bottom—totally weird. "Follow me," he says and rocks back and forth out of the room.

Me and Charlie grab my stuff and scurry to catch up with Mc-Steel. He looks back at us over his shoulder. "Air awareness," he mutters and leads us up the stairs to the trampoline. "Get in there and let me see you jump," he says to me, waving his hand back and forth toward the trampoline. I climb in and start jumping. "Good," McSteel grunts, "now let me see you spin." He points his index finger toward the ceiling and rotates his hand around in a circle. "Spin around once." I spin. "Now give me two spins." I try, but I can't do it. "Okay, stop right there," he says and waves me over to the edge of the trampoline. "Two things I want you to think about. One—pull your knees up to your chest as soon as your feet leave the surface. Two—cock your shoulder way back and as soon as you're up in the air, throw it around as hard as you can in the direction you want to spin. He holds up his fingers. "Two things—now go ahead and do it."

I walk back out to the center whispering to myself, "Knees,

shoulders, knees, shoulders." I take a deep breath and start bouncing. I do exactly what he tells me and pull off a double spin, no problem. Then McSteel tosses me the funny-looking skate deck that doesn't have any wheels. "Slide your feet through the straps and start jumping."

At first it feels kinda weird, but once I get used to it, it's totally cool. McSteel has me jump with the deck strapped to my feet and practice all kinds of different grabs. Then we start on the spins. "Spinning's all about shoulders. Pull the knees up and throw the shoulders. Now let me see you do it," he barks. I position myself in the middle of the trampoline and practice rotating around in the air with the board strapped to my feet and I got it. I know I'm gonna be able to pull all sorts of sick tricks on the vert ramp. McSteel calls me over. "Hop outta there and let me see you drop in on the big ramp," he grumbles.

I slide into my knee pads, pop a helmet on my head, and get set up at the top of the vert ramp.

McSteel looks at me. "Don't try nothing fancy. I just wanna see ya air outta the thing, that's all."

I nod, stomp on the front of my board, and drop in. As soon as I approach the coping I suck my knees into my chest and fly out of the ramp as high as I can. I rotate around, spot my landing, reenter the ramp, and pop out on the deck I started on.

"Do it a few more times," McSteel orders. So I keep skating, getting air and messing around with simple grab tricks. McSteel wags a finger in my direction. "That's enough for today," he says. He leans over, says something to Charlie, then turns around, grabs the handrail, and lumbers down the stairs.

"What'd he say?" I ask.

"Says you get good boost out of the ramp—that he's gonna teach you a nine hundred—two and half rotations," he says, spinning his finger in the air two and a half times.

The old man's walking below us. From the top deck I see him rocking back and forth toward the hallway. I hang my body over the railing. "Thanks for helping me, Mr. McSteel," I call after him.

"Call me Steely," he shouts back without turning around to look in my direction, his voice bouncing off the walls and echoing through the compound as he leaves the room.

ABSOLUTELY TRUE DIARY OF A PART-TIME SKATER

Piles of new ADSK gear sit in every corner of my bedroom. My mom helps me put my old clothes in boxes under my bed and we put all my new stuff on hangers in my closet. Cody comes over and laughs at my buzz cut. He hangs out with me while I put brand-new ADSK ball caps in rows in my chest of drawers. I even take down my old poster of Danny Way—the one where he's airing over the Great Wall of China. I roll it up and stash it under my bed along with all of my other stuff and then Cody helps me hang a cool new poster on my bedroom wall that I scored from the ADSK board room. I hook Cody up, shove a bunch of ADSK T-shirts and ball caps into his arms, and then we bolt down the stairs and charge the buttery half-pipe that's sitting in my backyard waiting to be ridden.

"What's it like?" Cody asks before he sets his board on the coping and gets ready to drop in.

"What's what like?"

"I don't know, being sponsored and stuff."

"It's sick," I say. "Wish I could skate the training facility with you and Niko. Some dumb rule—only ADSK team riders allowed."

"It's cool." He drops into the half-pipe and starts pumping up the walls. "Nothing wrong with your backyard and the skate park," he shouts.

"Yeah, for sure," I say, watching him grind across the coping.

We play a long game of skate and then the horn of Cody's mom's car blurts from my driveway. Cody pops his board into his hand, grabs his backpack, and we head through my house toward the front door. As he hops in the car I shout, "You at your mom's or dad's house this weekend?"

"Dad's," he hollers back.

"You, me, and Niko will skate when you get back, then."

Cody grins, gives me a thumbs-up, and then his mom backs the car down our driveway.

I session on the half-pipe for a little while, until my dad calls me in for dinner. My mom, dad, little brother, and me are sitting around the dinner table and I'm laying into my food when my dad drops a bomb. "Josh, we have to talk," he says. Mikey stops gnawing on the chicken leg he's devouring and looks at me.

"My grades are fine," I say, between mouthfuls of mashed potatoes.

"It's not your grades," my mom says.

I stop eating, chew on my bottom lip for a second because I'm not really sure what's going on. My mom picks up her fork. "I can't keep driving you to skate practice five days a week." She sighs.

Then my dad jumps in. "It's an hour and a half there and back, and Mom can't sit there for *three hours* while you skate. She has work. Deadlines. I'm sorry, son, but your skate schedule isn't working out for the family."

My mom moves a mound of steamed broccoli around on her plate. "Josh, we know how important this ADSK skating thing is to you, but . . ."

I put my fork down. "How about we buy me a car," I say, looking at both of them, begging, pleading with my eyes. "You could give me a loan until I save up my ADSK money."

"You know we can't afford that right now. Hannah's in college. I'll tell you what we can do. We can buy you a bus pass," my dad says.

"A bus pass? The bus? That's it? So you're not saying I have to quit ADSK?"

"Sweetheart, all we're saying is that if you want to keep skating, you're going to have to figure out a way to get yourself to and from the training facility." My mom picks up a bowl and passes it to my dad.

"A bus pass," I whisper to myself.

"Guess what I learned today?" Mikey pipes in out of nowhere.

"What did you learn, Mikey?" my mom asks.

"This guy named Van Go really loved to paint, and guess what he did? He cut off his ear."

My dad slices the meat on his plate. "Sometimes a person has to suffer for his art," he says, glancing my way.

"I'd rather just draw pictures." Mikey shrugs and starts chomping on his chicken leg again.

I take a deep breath and move some food around with my fork before I start eating again. It's quiet until everyone's finished their dinner. I help clear the table and then go upstairs to my room to finish my homework.

After school I sit on the old bench on the curb next to Federico's Taco Shop and wait for the bus. It's my new ritual. Every day. Five days a week. Me on the city bus heading to the ADSK training facility. It takes a *long* time to get there, but the training facility, also known as the TF, is *so rad* that I'd sit on a bus forever if that's what it took to get there. At first I listen to music and read skate magazines, and then I start my homework so I don't have to stay up so late studying once I get home.

My English teacher, Mr. Cunningham, a pretty cool guy who's crazy about books, makes our whole class read this book called *Absolutely True Diary of a Part-Time Indian*. I actually like it because it has all these cool drawings and the guy telling the story, Arnold Jr., is funny—not like that Holden dude in our last book who complained about everything. Anyway, Mr. Cunningham says that even though we think people might be 100 percent different from us, sometimes you can find things that you have in common, so for homework we have to read the book about Arnold and compare ourselves with what he's going through.

At first I think the assignment's going to be really hard, because the kid telling the story is a Native American Indian who lives on a reservation in the middle of nowhere and he has it rough . . . *really rough*, and I'm this kid living with my mom and dad in a two-story house with a half-pipe in my backyard, so I don't think we're similar at all. But then I think about it and I think Mr. Cunningham might be right—me and Arnold *do* have some things in common.

I mean, Arnold's crazy about basketball and I'm crazy about skating. And Arnold has this dream, right?—something he really wants to do—so he decides to go to school really far away from where he lives and he has to walk or get a ride super far every day. And even though I know I don't have it nearly as bad as Arnold, I have a dream too, something I really want to do, and I'm taking a bus for hours. But it's not that we're both obsessed, or that we both have a dream, or that we both have to travel far away from where we live to go after our dreams. The *biggest* thing we have in common is Arnold loses his best friend, and I know *exactly* what that's like, because I lost my best friend too. And the thing is, even though me and Brendon don't even talk anymore, even though he turned out to be a complete jackass, I *still* miss him.

I start filling in the circle diagram thing that we have to do for homework where we write down how we're the same and how we're different. It's a lot easier than I thought it would be. And just as I'm finishing the assignment, the bus finally gets to my stop a block away from the training facility, so I throw my stuff into my backpack, grab my board, and hop off the bus.

I cruise into the TF and get ready to warm up on the vert ramp. I'm wrestling with my knee pad trying to get it to fit over my pant leg when some skater cruises over to where I'm sitting. I look up. "You're Lowman, right—the new guy?" he says. I nod, totally speechless. He stretches out his balled-up hand and gives me a fist bump. "I'm Taj." He waves his thumb toward a guy skating behind us. "That fool over there is Ricky. We're gonna session here too if you don't mind."

"No worries," I sputter. He skates away and I sit there dumbstruck. Taj Roberts and Ricky Rodriguez totally dominate Gruel TV. Photos of them absolutely shredding are featured in every skate magazine around the world. I finish getting my gear on and head over to the ramp. I watch Ricky skate. Boosting out of the ramp, he grabs the nose of his board and arcs through the air, reenters smooth like butter, flies through the bottom and up the next wall, kickflips into a back lip on the coping, slides and rolls away, totally in control. Taj nods at me, signaling that he wants me to go.

I take a deep breath and drop in. I speed through the bottom of the ramp, race up the giant vertical wall in front of me, scoop the board up, and pull my knees into my chest. I press the board to my feet with my back hand, my front hand stretched out in front of me like the wing of a 747 airplane, and I'm soaring. I rotate my body 180 degrees while I'm up in the air, spot the landing, and burst back into the ramp. Popping out the other side, I catch my board in my hand and land with both feet planted firmly on the top platform. I don't pull anything fancy, but I know I got a huge amount of air. Taj whistles. Ricky looks at me and nods, then he drops in and we take turns skating the vert ramp until Steely wobbles up the stairs and motions me over to the trampoline.

I turn to Taj and Ricky. "Later," I say, brushing the sweat from my brow.

"Later," they answer back.

"Hey, Lowman," Taj hollers as I walk away. "See you around."

Steely gets me going on the trampoline and we follow our routine. I jump and spin with the deck of a skateboard attached to my feet while Steely stands on the sidelines coaching me. "Throw the shoulders, drive the hips," he repeats over and over until I hear it in my head even when he's not saying anything at all. He looks at me without speaking for a second, then grunts, "Control. You gotta learn to control yourself up there." He points his finger upward. He makes me do slow spins and fast spins, encouraging me to feel the difference between the two, and talks to me about feeling where I'm at when I'm up in the air.

Steely gestures for me to get off the trampoline. We head over to the empty vert ramp, where Steely has me drop in on the opposite side of the foam pit. He has me speed down the first wall, race up the second, boost into the air, and spin as many times as I can before landing in the foam. I do it over and over until I can spin three rotations easily. After a while Steely can tell that I'm beat. "That's enough for today, see you tomorrow," he bellows before swaying from side to side down the stairs.

I sit on the edge of the ramp for a while, until I muster the strength to walk down the stairs, drop down next to my backpack, and slide out of my stinky, sweaty pads one by one. Eventually I gather up my stuff and drag myself over to the bus stop. The sun, a glowing orange ball in the distance, slides behind foothills, and backlit ribbons of skinny clouds streak through the sky. As I plop down on the bench, streetlamps flicker on one by one down the long boulevard. I throw my head back, close my eyes, and even though I'm not moving I feel like my body is floating through the air. A car revs its engine close to me. I open my eyes. Dirk Davies sits in his car at the curb. "That you, Josh?" he asks through the rolled-down passenger window.

I nod. "Hey, Mr. Davies, how's it going?"

"What are you doing here?"

"Waiting for the bus."

"Long bus ride back to Green Valley," he says.

"Yeah." I take a quick glance down the boulevard.

"Well, see you at the TF tomorrow then." He flashes me a peace sign and races away.

I sit on the bench, daylight slowly fading, until the bus finally pulls up to the curb and screeches to a stop. I hop on. Except for a few weary people slumped against the backrests of hard plastic seats, the bus is empty. I take my place by a window toward the back. Fishing around in my backpack, I take out my book. The bus crawls slowly through the twilight and I try to read, but with every inch of my body tired to the bone, and the low hum of the bus engine reverberating up through the floorboards, I slowly drift off to sleep.

9

SECRETS

Erin calls me on the telephone and she's so excited I think she might've just won a million dollars. "You're not gonna believe it," she says. "I made the soccer team!"

"No way. That's awesome!" I say.

There's this kind of awkward pause and then Erin says, "Sorry I missed your birthday yesterday. I've just been crazy busy."

I hold my temporary license above me as we talk, tilt it back and forth in the stream of sunlight that filters through my window, still not believing that it's mine. "No worries," I say. "Guess what? My mom took me for my driver's test and I passed. I can drive."

"No way," she says. "We need to celebrate. Let's go to Federico's for some tacos this weekend."

"Sounds good to me," I say and hang up the phone.

When Saturday finally rolls around me and Erin have to walk to the taco shop 'cause my mom says she's busy and can't lend me our piece-of-crap mini van. For some reason Erin's acting weird and makes us take the long way into town. We cruise the alleys and side streets and finally land at Federico's ready to lay into some serious Mexican food. We order our stuff and sit down in one of the orange booths when I notice Brendon's initials carved into the table from a long time ago. I point it out to Erin.

"Hey," she says, "did I tell you I saw him at the ADSK Skate Jam thingy you won? He was there with a bunch of his new friends. He didn't look good."

"Whaddya mean?"

"He just looked different."

I rub my hand over my soft spiky hair. "Different, huh?"

"Well . . . I mean, you know . . . there's different good and different bad."

"Which one was he?"

"Different bad . . . definitely different bad."

"Which one am I?"

But before she can answer the dude that took our order calls our names. I pop up, grab our food, and sit back down. Erin reaches over, tries to pluck her rolled tacos from the tray, but I pull them back before she can get to them.

"Hold on a second." I stand up on the booth bench, lift her tacos into the air, and clear my throat. "Ladies and gentlemen," I bellow. "A toast to my friend Erin . . . a great girl . . . who just made the soccer team at Valley View High and . . . who is destined to be rad and kick some serious butt this season." Smiling, I hop down and take a bow. A few people in the corner booths start clapping. Erin shakes her head laughing, I hand her stuff over, and she digs in. One of the things I like about Erin the most—she's not afraid to really dive into her food.

We sit there chowing down when the door swings open. I look up. Matthew Cuttahy strolls in with two of his friends. He sees Erin and walks over to our table. "Hey, Erin." He nods in my direction. "Hey," he says.

I nod back and keep chewing slowly. Erin sets down her taco. Grabbing a napkin, she wipes her mouth while Matthew Cuttahy stands there talking to her. "Congratulations. Heard you made the soccer team," he says.

"Yeah, I'm really happy." Erin brushes a piece of her hair behind her ear.

"Well, you should be." He looks at me and then flips his car keys around his finger. He nods at Erin. "See you later." He walks over to the counter and orders lunch with his friends.

Erin picks up her rolled tacos. Cuttahy and his pals get their order to go and split. She watches them. As soon as they leave and the door closes behind them, she dives back into her food.

When we're finished eating, we both sit there quiet for a second. Erin sips her drink and I kind of poke at the rest of the food that's on my plate. Finally I look across the table at her. "Do you like him?" I ask.

"Who?" She plays with the straw in her drink, and then starts tracing her finger over the graffiti on the table.

"Matthew Cuttahy."

"He's nice."

"That's not what I mean."

She quits tracing the initials carved into the table and looks at me.

"I mean, you know . . . do you like like him?" I ask.

She picks up her drink again, smiling. "Are you jealous?"

"Of what? Him? You gotta be kiddin' me. I just wanna know if you like him?"

"Do I like him? Hmmm, well let's see . . . I think he's . . . nice."

"So you do then, you do like him? Come on, you can tell me,

we're best friends!" I say.

She kicks my foot under the table. "No way, not telling," she says, and then she goes back to the scrawled designs in the table. "So . . . who do *you* like?" she asks, drawing invisible pictures with her index finger on the bright-orange tabletop.

"No one."

She looks up. "Come on, Josh, you can tell me, you gotta like someone."

"Not telling."

Tapping the table lightly with both hands, she leans in toward me. "Well then, looks like we both have secrets," she whispers. A half smile glued to her face, she stands up, clears the wrappers and food scraps off the table, plops them in the trash can, and we leave.

We head back to my house. Erin makes us take the long way again. She walks real slow and keeps stopping to point out squirrels in trees and dogs in backyards and cats napping under parked cars in people's driveways and right before we get to my front door, she hunches over. "Stupid pebble." She looks up at me. "Go ahead and go inside," she says, fumbling with her shoe. She's crouched down, staring at me with a funny look in her eyes. "Go on, I'll be right there," she insists. Tilting my head, I turn around, open the door, and I'm practically knocked over by a sound wave of people shouting "SURPRISE!" I jump back and stare into my living room. A pack of family and friends stand together, hooting and laughing, the high-pitched squeak of noisemakers blasting through the room. I look around, totally shocked. Niko, Cody, Big Chad, and Zander emerge from the crowd and give me high fives. A couple of my other skater friends from the Green Valley Skatepark come up and bump my fist, and my big sister, Hannah, appears out of nowhere and hugs me.

My mom clicks pictures on her camera. My dad stands behind her, his arms folded across his chest, smiling. I look back at Erin. A huge smile spreads across her face. I shake my head. "You guys got me," I say. Then I lock my eyes on Erin. "Thought you forgot."

She shrugs. "Secrets," she says. Laughing, she grabs my arm and leads me into the house.

A big banner sways across the patio doors. HAPPY 16TH BIRTH-DAY, it says in big bold letters. My dad bolts into the backyard, scrambles around the barbecue grilling up burgers and dogs, and my mom mills around making sure everyone's happy. She catches me standing in the middle of a group of friends, listening but mostly staring at the half-pipe in our backyard. "Why don't you guys go out back and skate," she hollers, looking at me and winking.

A bunch of us grab boards and head out to the half-pipe. We play a long game of skate before my mom calls everyone back into the house. My friends push me through the patio doors and as soon as I pass through the doorway, my mom walks toward me with a giant lit-up birthday cake. Everyone in the whole room sings "Happy Birthday" at the top of their lungs. I get a huge slab of cake and go sit next to Erin on a picnic bench in our backyard. We sit underneath a thousand twinkling stars, so close that our legs are touching, so close that I can smell the scent of vanilla lotion floating from her skin. "Happy birthday, Josh," she says and I feel like whispering in her ear, asking her one more time, *Who do you like, Erin, who is it?* But it feels so nice sitting this close to her and I don't want to ruin a perfect day.

10

CONTROL AND TIMING

When I'm in class listening to teachers lecture about stuff I don't really care about, my mind wanders and the next thing I know I'm skating in my head. All I can think about is pulling the 900. I'm dropping in and boosting into the air. The nose of my board is skyrocketing out of the ramp, so I twist my torso back, throw my shoulders around just like Steely taught me, and bam, I complete one full spin, 360 degrees, *but* with one full spin, the nose of my board's still facing *out* of the ramp. Two full spins, 720 degrees, and the nose of my board is *still* heading toward the moon. So I squeeze half a rotation more in there. I tack on 180 degrees to my two full spins so that now, the nose of my board is facing back *into* the ramp and I can pull the landing, because with a 900 it's not so much about spinning around in the air, it's about spinning around exactly two and a half times. It's about reentering the ramp heading in the right direction. It's about the landing. And in my head, I land it every time.

When I'm not dreaming about skating, I'm thinking about Steely's words, which I can't get out of my head. He tells me that it doesn't matter if I can spin fifty rotations when I'm jumping on the trampoline, or flying out of the vert ramp and landing in the foam pit. I have to *feel* where my body's at when I'm up in the air. I have to learn *control*. So we play this game when I'm jumping on the trampoline or landing in the foam pit. He calls out the number of spins he wants me to do as soon as my feet leave the surface.

"Three sixty," he rasps. I adjust my body, throw my shoulders just right, and bust out one spin. "Seven twenty," he hollers. I have to throw my shoulders to initiate the spin and tuck into a tight ball all at the same time, *and* I have to spin faster than when I'm doing a 360 because I only have so much time up in the air before I come crashing back down. "Controlled spins." That's what Steely calls it. It's almost become normal for me to walk around mumbling to myself, "Three sixty, seven twenty, drive your hips, throw your shoulders, control the spin," as if Steely has taken up permanent residence between my ears.

Most of the time my body's so sore I can barely move, because every day I do a bunch of leg squats and sit-ups, *and* I ride the vert ramp to work on getting as much height and boost out of the coping as humanly possible. When I ask Steely why he's making me do all this stuff, he says, "You strip a nine hundred down to its bare essentials, it's about control and timing. You remember that"—he wags a gnarled finger at my chest—"control and timing." And it becomes the saying that I repeat in my head the most, over and over—when I'm on the bus, sitting in class, eating breakfast, I hear Steely's words, "control and timing." And when I'm lying in bed at night, I can still feel my body moving like I'm on a skateboard. I lie there perfectly still and I can feel myself floating through the air, spinning, the words "control and timing" a continuous loop playing in my head before I drift off to sleep.

When I walk into the TF, my sore muscles are starting to loosen up a bit and Steely's words are ringing in my head. I session with Taj and Ricky on the indoor street course until I see Steely waiting for me at the top of the vert ramp. "Over here, kid," he hollers. "Get on the trampo and start warming up." I stash my board under a bench, hustle over, and get started. Steely leans against the rail and watches me jump. "What are ya thinking about?" he shouts.

"Control and timing," I say between jumps.

"Atta boy." Steely nods, then waves me over to the vert ramp and for the first time ever, he cracks a smile.

I slide on my pads, pop on my helmet, grab my board, and bolt up the stairs. He grabs my shoulders, stares at me in the eyes. "You're ready," he says. "You're ready to finally try the nine. First few runs, get warmed up. Nothin' fancy."

I drop in a couple of times and get big air, nice and high out of the ramp. Steely stands on the platform. His arms crossed against his enormous barrel chest, he nods . . . satisfied. Finally he uncrosses his arms, rubs his hands together. "It's time," he announces, his voice bouncing off the walls of the warehouse.

Standing at the top of the ramp, I stare down the steep vertical wall. "Control, timing, control, timing," I repeat to myself and drop in. I race down the first wall, fly up the second, set my shoulders and as soon as I'm in the air I tuck into a tight ball, whip my shoulders around, and spin. I'm trying to feel the timing, hoping to spot the landing through the blur, but I get kind of lost up there and I know it's not right. I huck my board away from my body and move my legs like I'm running through air. Finally, I figure out where the ramp is, tuck my knees underneath me, land on my knee pads, and slide down the steep wall until I come to a stop. I stand up, shake it off, and look up. Steely stands at the edge of the ramp peering down at me. "You all right?" he asks. I nod. "Good, now get up here and do it again," he barks.

I clutch my board by the trucks and head back up to the top. I spend the whole afternoon trying to pull a 900, getting closer and closer each time, but still no luck. I want to pull it *so bad*, I'd skate till midnight if Steely would let me, but he makes me pack it up and head home after about three hours of trying. I'm sitting on the bench at the bottom of the vert ramp, sliding out of my pads, sweaty and tired and frustrated. Steely rocks over, shoves his hands into his pockets, and stands over me in silence. He stares at me with his fierce blue eyes. "Don't give up," he whispers. "You hear me? Don't give up," and then he turns and walks away.

For a whole week, I drop into the ramp, set my hips, throw my shoulders, spin through the air, and I'm close, I'm *so* close, but I just can't nail the landing. On Friday I take off my helmet, huck my board across the warehouse, grind my teeth, and look at Steely. "I'm done," I say. "I'm over it."

Steely looks at me, slowly shaking his head. "It's part of the deal, kid. Anything worth landing takes time." He points a gnarled finger toward the stairs. "Now get up there. Quit whining."

I inhale and blow out a loud sigh. I gather my board, plop my helmet on my head, and drag myself up the stairs. I stand at the top of the vert ramp and stare across to the opposing wall. I take a deep breath and drop in. I launch into the air, press my board to my feet with my back hand, throw my shoulders, spin around once, twice, half a rotation more and I'm high enough in the air that I have time to complete the two and a half rotations. I spot the landing before swooshing back into the ramp, the clunk of my wheels smacking against the smooth wood of the steep wall. And finally, the skate gods smile down on me from the heavens above; finally, I *land* a 900. I slide to my knees, not really sure if I should laugh or cry, so I let out a giant whoop instead, pop up to my feet, and look up toward Steely. He's standing at the edge of the ramp, pumping his fist in the air. "Atta boy, Josh. Atta boy! Now get up here and do it again!" he hollers.

I race back to the top of the ramp and keep skating. I land a clean 900 *three times* before Steely calls it a day. I head down to the bottom of the ramp, sit on a bench, and gulp down a cold bottle of water. Steely walks over. Placing a leathery hand on my shoulder, he stands there for a second, nods slowly, and then spins around and wobbles out of the warehouse. I watch him sway back and forth as he leaves the room.

I take off my pads, sweaty and tired and satisfied, then gather up my stuff before heading toward the exit. Right before I reach the door, I notice a shadow spilling onto the concrete of the warehouse floor. I glance over. Dirk's leaning against the wall of the hallway. He doesn't say anything. Standing there, he studies me, and I can feel his eyes on my back as I walk out the door.

11

SECRET WEAPON

I walk into the training facility on Monday, grab the wheel-less skate deck, and head over to the trampoline to get warmed up, but before I get there Steely shakes his head and sweeps his hand back and forth in the air motioning toward the ADSK offices that line the hallway. "Dirk wants to see you in his office," he grumbles.

"What for?" I ask.

Steely shrugs. "Dunno. I'll be in the board room. Come and get me when you're ready to skate," he says, then turns around and splits.

I walk toward the hallway, my mind racing because I'm not stupid. I know that getting called into the office always sucks. The principal or vice principal wants to see you because your grades are in the toilet, or you're tardy all the time, or some cranky teacher saw you commit the crime of the century, like riding your skateboard down the hall on the way to class. So I shuffle through the TF toward Dirk's office trying to remember if I did anything wrong.

When I get there, Dirk's sitting in an enormous swivel chair talking on the phone. He motions for me to come into the room and sit in the chair facing his desk. He's barking orders into the phone at someone while I sit there checking out the room. Pictures of a bunch of different ADSK pros hang on the wall. Right smack in the center, he has a giant photo of himself in a fancy suit, staring straight into the camera, his white teeth gleaming. He's shaking his one hand with some old politician dude and holding a giant pair of scissors in the other getting ready to cut a giant ribbon strung across the entryway to the ADSK TRAINING FACILITY AND WARE-HOUSE.

Dirk, clicking the phone down, swivels his head over his shoulder to see what I'm looking at. He swings back around to face me. "That's me in the beginning," he says. He gestures toward the wall behind him. "How'd you like to have your picture hanging back there?"

I swallow, praying that my voice won't crack. "I'd like it," I say.

He laughs, "Well good, because I think you're on your way. I like you, Josh. You remind me of myself—a hard worker."

I breathe. Not tardy, not busted. Not in trouble. "Thanks," I say.

Dirk clicks the pen he's holding in his hand. "You know, I think you might be our secret weapon. Steely tells me you've been skating hard. Practicing a lot. That you have the nine hundred on lock. Landed it clean a few times in practice."

I nod.

"That's great, Josh. I can't even tell you how great." Dirk smiles.

"Thanks." I put my hands in my pocket and shuffle around in my seat.

Dirk sets the pen down. "So, here's what we're going to do. It's time to introduce *Josh Lowman, ADSK secret weapon*, to the world." He rests his folded hands on the giant desk in front of him. "I just got off the phone with the top skating magazine in the industry. They're going to run a feature article on you."

"You're kidding," I mutter.

"Nope, not kidding. A photographer's going to come out to get some shots of you skating. I want Taj and Ricky in on the shoot too—maximum exposure." He grins. "They'll send a writer over to interview you, *and* it gets even better." He swivels in his chair, opens a mini fridge behind him, pops open a chilled can of Godzilla sports drink, and slides it to me across the desk. "Heard of the Godzilla Vert Series?" he asks.

I shake my head.

He grabs a water bottle out of the fridge and takes a swig. "Godzilla sports drinks is hosting a series of vert competitions. First stop is here at the TF; then the series moves up the state and across the nation. No one's ever pulled a nine hundred in competition, Josh . . . no one. And the first one to do it is going be you— an Alpha Dog team rider. It's going to go off the Richter scale. Every skater in the world is going to want Alpha clothes, Alpha boards, Alpha everything!" His eyes glisten as he talks. "I need you out here skating six days a week, Monday through Saturday. What do you think?"

"Uh . . . I guess . . . but . . ."

"But what? What's the problem?"

"It's just—the bus. Six days a week. It sucks up a lot of time."

"Oh yeah, the bus. I already thought about that." He stands up grinning, opens a drawer to his desk, pulls something out, and clenches it in his balled-up fist so I can't see what he's holding. "Follow me," he says. We walk down the hall in silence. Dirk leads me to a giant metal door at the back of the warehouse and pushes it open. We pop out into the sunlight. "I just got a new car a few months ago and I don't have the heart to sell my first true love. It's been sitting here gathering dust." He points to a car at the far end of the lot.

Dirk spins a set of keys around on his index finger, catches them in his hand, then tosses them to me. "Here you go," he says. "Use some of the money I'm paying you for gas and insurance and I'll loan it to you. Time to throw away your bus pass." He crosses his arms across his chest, rocks back and forth on his feet, and smiles.

"I can't believe it," I sputter.

"Believe it. You're part of the Alpha team. We take care of each other." He slaps my shoulder, then nods toward the warehouse. "Now go grab Steely and get some skating in. Godzilla competition is just around the corner. We've got work to do." He spins around on his heels and heads back into the TF.

I stare at the keys in my hand, my mouth gaping open. I bolt over to the far parking spot and stand next to the sickest Ford Mustang I've ever seen in my life. I look in the windows, put my hand on the hood of the car, open the door and peer inside. I can't wait to pick up Cody and Niko and cruise around in search of epic skate spots. I can't wait to see the expression on my mom and dad's faces when I pull into our driveway. But most of all, I can't wait to take Erin Campbell for a spin in my sweet new ride.

12

MORP

I dip into buffing wax with my mitted fingers, brush my palm in wide circles, dig into every groove, slide my hand along the curves and lines of Dirk's fine automobile, which is *my* fine automobile for now, until it sparkles and shines. I even spray stuff on the wheels so that the whitewall stripes are spotless and the black tarry background of the tires glimmers in the sun. And then I call Erin, ask her to meet me in front of her house. I hop in the driver's seat, turn the key, and smile. Elbow resting on the frame of my rolled-down window, hand resting on the steering wheel, tunes blasting from the stereo, I cruise over to Erin's in total style.

I pull into her driveway. Wearing soccer shorts and a T-shirt, she sits cross-legged on the grass in her front yard, reading a book. She looks over, but she can't see that it's me through the tinted glass. I roll down the passenger window. "What's up?" I shout. "Wanna go for a ride?"

Craning her neck in my direction, she looks over. "Josh?" Tossing her book down, she stands up. "Is that you?"

"It's me, all right. Hop in. Let's go for a ride," I say, smiling.

She walks over and leans through the passenger window. "Where'd you get it?"

"Dirk Davies from ADSK. He's letting me use it so I don't have to take the bus anymore. Come on. Get in. Let's go get a slushie." I rev the engine a few times and we both crack up.

She hops in and we pull out of the driveway. Wind rushes in from the rolled-down windows, and music blasts from the radio. I feel like my face is going to split in half from the huge smile plastered there. We pull into the mini mart parking lot, hop out and head into the store, racing to the slushie machine to see who gets there first.

"Go for the biggest one and get one of those licorice straws too if you want," I say. "I'm buying." We elbow each other, pushing each other out of the way to get at the best flavors. She karate kicks me a couple of times, and her soccer legs are strong and lethal.

We're giggling and wrestling and pouring our slushies when someone calls our names. "Hey, Josh . . . Erin." We both turn around at the same time. It's Brendon. Under the fluorescent lights of the mini mart he looks horrible, so bad I hardly recognize him. Big dark circles camp out under his eyes. His skin is so pasty white it's practically translucent. A long-sleeved, flannel shirt hangs from his too-skinny torso, and strands of greasy hair stick to his hollow face.

"Brendon, is that you?" I ask, hardly able to believe the ghost of Brendon Johnson standing before me. "You look so . . . different," I whisper.

His hands in his pockets, he glances up from the ground, kind of laughing. "So do you," he says.

"You been skating much?" I ask, not really sure what else to say since I haven't seen him since the trial.

"Nah. Sold my boards." He shuffles around on the shiny floor. "Needed money." He looks over his shoulder toward the exit, then turns back to face us. "Hey man," he says, practically whispering, "could you do me a favor? Could you lend me a couple bucks?" He pushes his hands deeper into his pockets.

I'm frozen for a second, looking at Brendon who's staring at his feet, and then finally I take out my wallet and hand him five dollars. Reaching out to grab the money, his pale hand trembles under the bright lights. "Thanks, man," he says. Clutching the bill in his wobbly hand, he turns around and slinks out of the store.

Erin and me look at each other, then finish filling up our cups in silence. We hop in my car, drive over to the Green Valley Skatepark, and park under the orange glow of humming night-lights, the silhouette of the vert ramp barely visible through the darkness. I stare straight ahead, drinking my slushie, a song I don't recognize seeping through the speakers. I can't talk because of the lump in my throat. Erin sets down her drink, shuts off the radio, and looks at me. "Josh," she says.

"What *happened* to him?" I sigh. "He was my *best* friend."

"Whatever's going on with Brendon has nothing to do with you."

I swallow. Clench my teeth. Try to hold it together. "Let's get out of here." I start the engine and we leave.

Driving around the streets of Green Valley, I catch a glimpse of Erin in the corner of my eye. She rests her head against the back of her seat, closes her eyes, smiles. The breeze rushing through the windows brushes against her smooth skin. We swing by her place, grab a soccer ball, and go to Old Oaks Park. We jump out of the car, the slamming of the car door the only sound that echoes through the empty grass field. We kick the ball back and forth across fresh-cut grass, both of us hypnotized by the rhythm of our bodies moving in the darkness, until Erin stops the ball with her foot. "Isn't it funny?" she says, "How so much has changed?"

"Whaddya mean?" I ask.

"Well, I was friends with Brendon before I was friends with you, and back when we were in ninth grade sitting in English class, if you would've told me we'd be best friends, I'd never have believed it. And now here we are kicking a ball together in the dark and I'm on the soccer team and you're a sponsored skater. I mean, it's kind of crazy, don't you think?"

I nod and plop down on the grass.

Erin sits down across from me and hugs her knees to her chest. "Hey," she says, "did you hear about the MORP dance at our school?"

I shake my head.

"Well, it spells *prom* backward, so it's a backward dance. So girls ask guys and I'm asking you. Let's go. It'll be fun"

"To a dance?"

"Yeah, to the backward dance."

I nod, thinking about Brendon, his skin as pale as a ghost's, his hand shaking, him standing there looking like a shell of the person he used to be. "It'd be cool to go backward," I say. "When's the dance?"

"Two weeks from this Saturday. My first soccer game of the season's that same afternoon."

"I'll go." I nod slowly. "I'll go to your game, too."

"Great." Smiling, she stands up. "Come on," she says. "We better get out of here . . . curfew."

We head to her house. I pull into the driveway and park. She reaches around, grabs her soccer ball from the backseat, and hops out of the car. "Hey, Erin," I say.

She leans through the passenger window. "Yeah?"

I look straight into her green eyes. "Thanks."

She smiles, turns, and walks away. I take a deep breath and exhale, watching her float through the porch lights and walk through her front door.

13

THE WRONG GUY

Right when I walk into the training facility, Charlie rushes over and grabs me by the arm. "Big day for you, dude," he says. "Hope you're ready." He guides me to a corner of the TF where some lady puts face powder stuff on poor Taj's face. Ricky sits there reading a magazine, waiting for his turn. "That's the stylist," Charlie whispers, motioning in the direction of the face-powder lady. "She's in charge of making you look good for the photo shoot."

Face-Powder Lady turns around. "Hi, I'm Kareen," she says, stretching out a hand with long red fingernails like cat claws.

"I'm Josh," I respond.

"Hi, Josh." She looks me up and down then focuses on my head. "Ewww. . . we really need to clean up that hair." She looks at her watch, then at Charlie. "What time's the shoot?"

"Half hour."

"Well, you're going to have to do something about his hair. I don't have time." She looks at me, Taj, and Ricky, shakes her head, then digs into a huge toolbox filled with all kinds of makeup stuff. Finally she pulls out a hair-clipper-razor thing and tosses it to Charlie.

He catches it in the air. "I can't do it. I was supposed to be in Dirk's office five minutes ago," he says, tossing the clippers to me.

"Have Steely give you a quick buzz. He's in the board room."

I stare at the thing in my hand. "You want me to ask Steely to give me a haircut?"

"Well . . . yeah." Charlie spins around and bolts toward Dirk's office.

"Great," I mutter under my breath.

I stand at the entrance to the board room. "Steely, you in here?" I shout. I hear some rustling around, then Steely emerges from his back office. "I'm here. You ready to skate?" he asks, eyeballing me.

"I wish. Photo shoot and, uh, well, Charlie asked me to ask you . . ."

"Yeah? What is it?"

"He asked you to give me a haircut," I say.

"Jeez." He shakes his head. "Whadda they think I'm running here, a beauty parlor?" He grabs the clippers. "Hop up here," he says, patting the counter. I jump up, get situated, and Steely starts buzzing away, but when he gets to the back of my head he clicks the razor off. "Holy Toledo, kid. What the heck happened to you here?" he says, tapping a finger on one of my scraggly scars. "Looks like you got in a fight with a jackhammer."

"I got hit."

"I'll say you got hit. What gotcha? A semi-truck?"

"A skateboard."

"A skateboard?" Steely, the clippers frozen in his hand, stands silent, waiting for an answer. I take a deep breath and blow out all the oxygen in my lungs. "This scumbag from the skate park went psycho," I say. "Totally lost it. Beat me with a skateboard. Skate trucks and skull bone. Not a good combination."

Steely takes a step closer, peers at the raised rivers of scars running along my scalp. "Jeez, he really tore into ya."

"Put me in intensive care. Traumatic brain injury. I was in a coma for a week. It was gnarly. That's what happened." I shrug.

"Brain injury?" He shakes his head. "Dirk know?"

"Nah. I don't really like to talk about it."

Steely glances over to the poster of himself when he was young, nodding slowly. "Better finish up here." He clicks the razor back on. When he's finally finished, I brush my hand over my fuzzy cranium. "Feels good," I say. Then a voice booms into the room from the intercom system. "Josh, get out to the floor. They're ready for you."

Steely puts his giant hand on my shoulder and grins. "Make sure you smile pretty for the camera, princess." He laughs deep from his belly and rocks back into his office.

I hurry out to the floor. Kareen, hands on her hips, stands there. She taps an empty chair, motioning for me to sit down. She dabs this crap on my face and practically kills me pulling out a few of my eyebrow hairs. Total torture. When she's done, she holds up a mirror. Studying my reflection, I hardly recognize the guy staring back at me. "Perfect," she says. "Exactly the look we're going for."

Rushing me out of the chair, she shoos me to the back of the warehouse where we pop out of a heavy metal door and enter into the bright daylight. It takes a few seconds for my eyes to adjust. When I finally focus, I see Dirk's brand-new, totally sick Corvette sitting in the middle of the parking lot with both doors open. Big mirror, light-catcher things rest on tripods and some guy, three enormous cameras slung around his neck, barks orders at his assistant. The camera dude turns to me. "You Josh?" he says.

"I think so," I stammer.

"Cool. I'm Dano." He shakes my hand. "I know. It looks like the set of a music video, right? Except today, I'm just shooting still photos. We'll do the live action shots inside on the skate ramps. Believe me. It's gonna be epic." He fidgets with one of the cameras dangling from his neck. "Okay. Let's get started." He waves his hand in the direction of the car. "Hop on the hood there, sit on the edge kinda with your feet on the bumper."

I hop up and do what he says.

"Perfect. Now take your arms and fold 'em across your chest. Yep, like that, that looks good." He gets me all adjusted, lifts one of the cameras to his eye. "Ready?" he asks.

"Ready," I say. I'm sitting on the hood of the car, my hands right where they should be, my head tilted just so. I bust out a smile, and wait for him to start clicking away.

He takes the camera from his face. "Ah, no. No, no, no. That's not what we're going for, Chief. Think alpha dog. Think top of the food chain. Just stare straight into the camera. No smile. Like you mean business."

So I give him my "alpha" face and he starts taking pictures, hopping around, adjusting, talking to himself. He calls Taj and Ricky over and has them stand next to the car doors, their feet planted shoulder distance apart, hands balled into fists resting on their hips. I'm on the hood of the car, with Taj and Ricky on each side, all of us looking straight into the camera with clenched jaws. Then Taj starts whispering jokes between shots, Ricky rips an enormous fart, and we can't keep it together. We *crack up*. The photographer dude leaps around snapping photos, begging us to be serious, to try to look tough, hollering at his assistant to grab more light here and place it there. It takes *forever*. Finally Dano lets us go into the training facility to get warmed up before he shoots us skating.

On the way into the TF, we duck into the bathroom and grapple over the sink to see who gets to rinse off first. I actually manage to get Taj in a headlock and almost shove Ricky into the urinal with my foot, so I'm the victor. I splash water all over—on my face, on my hair. It feels so good to get all of that makeup goop off me. Taj and Ricky take turns at the sink doing the same. We tumble out of the bathroom, shirts soaked, shoving each other, laughing, talking way too loud, when we run smack into Kareen. She takes one look at us and shakes her head. "You guys," she whines, "we're not done yet."

"Who cares? We're just skating," Ricky says. He shoves Taj into the wall. Taj kind of stumbles, looks at Kareen, shrugs, runs off. Ricky snatches me by the shirt and we chase after him.

We grab our boards and once we start skating, I lose all track of time. We session long and hard with Dano shooting us from every angle possible—from the bottom of the vert ramp, from the top, standing on a ladder. It takes *hours*. Finally Dano sets his camera down. "Okay, we're done here," he says. "Nice work."

Even after Dano clears all of his equipment and leaves, we stick around and skate the vert ramp and the street course until Taj hollers, "Let's get some chow."

"I'm in." Ricky nods. "Lowman, you come too." He pops his helmet off his head.

We toss our boards and helmets against a wall and walk a few blocks in the dark to the burger place just down the street. We order a mound of food and sit in a booth waiting for our order to arrive.

"Where you skate, Lowman?" Ricky asks.

"Dunno. Green Valley Skatepark. Street. Half-pipe in my backyard."

"Green Valley's sweet." Taj fumbles around with the plastic triangle that has our order number on it. "Let's skate it." He slams a fist on the table. "Tomorrow. You, me, and Ricky are skating the Green Valley vert ramp, *tomorrow*." He looks at Ricky, who's nodding in agreement. "We'll meet at the skate park at noon, skate our brains out and then chill," Taj says.

Ricky jabs a finger into my chest. "No flaking out either." He bumps my fist with his balled-up hand.

Finally our food comes. It's all hands and elbows going in for the kill until everyone gets what they ordered, then complete silence, except for the sound of three hungry skaters mowing their food. I take a big bite of my burger, stop chewing. "Wait a second," I say. "What day is it tomorrow?"

"Sunday," Taj and Ricky answer at the same time, their mouths full of food.

"So that means today is . . . *crap!*" Taj and Ricky quit eating and stare at me. "*Today's Saturday*," I blurt out. I look at my watch. Ten minutes to nine. "Erin . . . THE DANCE," I shout. I shove my food to the center of the table and stand up. "I gotta go. Crap. I gotta go right now."

"What's the matter with you?" Taj reaches for my fries and empties them onto his plate.

"See you tomorrow." I run out of the burger place as fast as I can. I try to get into the TF but it's locked and I don't have time to wait for someone to let me in. I fish my car keys out of my pocket, sprint to my car, and tear out of the parking lot. My heart's thumping hard against my chest and I'm praying that I make every green light. When I finally pull into Erin's driveway it's nine twenty. None of the lights are on anywhere in the house. I bolt to the front door and start ringing the bell and knocking until my knuckles hurt. No one's home. I get back in my car, slam my fist on the dashboard, groaning, and bury my face in my hands.

I sit there for a few minutes swearing at myself for being such an idiot and then I start the ignition and head over to the school. A glowing halo of light hovers over the gymnasium and I can hear music pulsating like a heartbeat as I park my car. I run to the front of the gym and when I finally catch my breath, a short, chubby lady working the entrance door looks at me shaking her head. "You're late," she says, a half smile spreading across her face.

"Yeah, I know," I say. "Really late."

"Well I'm sorry, but I can't let you in."

"Whaddya mean you can't let me in? You *have* to let me in. My friend, I mean, this girl. The girl I'm supposed to be with is in there without me."

"Can't let you in. Wish I could, but I can't. Doors closed half an hour ago. I'm just following orders, honey."

I can feel heat burning inside of me rising up into my chest. I look past the door lady, ready to barrel past her, when two burly dudes saunter over and stand next to the door too. Long thick beards flow from their chins, tattoos snake down their forearms, and red T-shirts with the word SECURITY in big white block letters on them cover their thick chests.

"Wish I could let you in, sweetheart. It's the school's policy, not mine," Door Lady says before I turn around and head back to my car.

I drive back to Erin's house and sit in her driveway hoping she shows up so I can explain. At five minutes to eleven, the house is still dark, still no Erin, and my parents' voices are ringing in my head grounding me forever if I don't get home by eleven o'clock curfew. I start the engine and slowly drive back to my house, wishing I could curl up into a ball and disappear.

In the morning the only thing I can think to do is go to her—go to her house and try to make her understand that it was a simple mistake. I roll out of bed, jump into some sweatpants, and drive over to her place. I stand at Erin's front door knocking and ringing the bell for a long time until she finally answers. She's in her PJs and her hair is kind of puffed up on one side. I get a little tongue-tied not exactly sure what to say, so I just stand there like an idiot with my hands in my pockets, staring at my toes squirming around in my flip-flops.

"Parents home?" I manage to blurt out.

"Church."

I nod. "Where were you last night? I waited here till eleven."

She laughs. "Where was *I*? . . . Where were *you*?"

"Look, Erin. *I'm sorry*," I say. "I was at this stupid photo shoot that took *forever*. Then me, Taj, and Ricky started skating, then we got hungry so we went to get some burgers and the next thing I know I look at my watch and it's like eight thirty. I just . . . I lost track of time."

She stands there staring into space.

"Erin?" I plead.

She leans against the doorjamb, twirling a strand of hair around her finger. "You were hanging out with your friends and you for-got. Forgot about me. Forgot about the dance."

"No, it's not like that." I stare at her, my heart beating louder and louder in my temples.

"I just asked the wrong guy, that's all. I should've never asked you in the first place," she whispers.

"No . . . you didn't . . . you didn't ask the wrong guy. You asked the right guy. Please don't say that, Erin. Please. You asked the right guy."

She shakes her head, and I'm not sure, but I think I see a tear slowly roll down her cheek. She swipes her hand across her face and then looks at me directly in the eyes.

What I should do, what I *really* want to do, is reach out and hold her close, tell her the truth, that she's the only girl who has ever mattered to me, ever, that I'm an idiot and I just screwed up. But I don't. I don't do it. "Well, where were *you*? I *waited*. I even went to the dance to try to find you and then I parked in your driveway and waited," I say.

"I was at the dance."

"*By yourself?*"

"No."

"Well, who'd you go with?"

"What's it matter?"

"Come on, tell me. I'm gonna find out at school. Just tell me."

She takes a deep breath, lets out a long sigh. She shifts her weight from one foot to the other. "Matthew."

"Matthew Cuttahy? *You went to the dance with Matthew Cuttahy?*"

"Well, I wanted to go with you, but you never showed up. What was I supposed to do?"

Then something inside of me snaps. My stomach burns, my temples pound, and I know I should keep my mouth shut, but I feel like a volcano erupting, spewing hot pools of molten lava into the atmosphere. "You like him. He's a total poser-wannabe-jock and you like him," I say.

"*No.*"

"Yes you do. Say it. You like him."

"No I don't. What are you mad at *me* for? I didn't do anything."

"Did you kiss him?"

"Josh, stop."

"You did, didn't you? You guys hooked up."

Erin shakes her head, her eyes smoldering like red-hot embers. "Why are you being such a jerk?"

"Admit it. You kissed him."

"Okay. Look. First of all, no, *I did not kiss him.* Second of all, even if I did, it's *none of your business. You're* the one who bailed on *me.*"

The way she looks at me makes my stomach burn even more and I wish so bad I could take back the words. "Erin, I . . ."

"You know what? Go ahead and hang out with your cool new skater friends. I don't even care anymore." She starts to shut the door, but pops her head out before it closes. "And one more thing—your 'new look,' the whole buzzed-haircut, tough-guy thing . . . it's really lame." Then she slams the door in my face.

I stand there, her front door about an inch from my nose. My hands shake and I'm sweating. Finally, I turn around, get in my car, and go back to my house.

I sit at the kitchen counter trying to eat a bowl of cereal when my mom walks in. "Hi, sweetie," she says. "What are you up to today?" She opens the fridge and looks around.

"Skating," I mumble, playing with the cereal floating around in my bowl.

"With Cody? He's called a few times."

"Nah, with a couple of guys from Alpha."

She closes the icebox, leans against the kitchen counter facing in my direction. "Well, you should call Cody back."

"Yeah, maybe later."

She studies me for a second. "You okay?" she asks, her mom-radar zeroing in on a vessel in distress.

"I'm fine."

"You sure?" She reaches across the counter and presses her hand to my forehead.

"Mom, I don't have a fever. I'm fine." I stand up and put my bowl in the sink.

"Okay, well, I'm going to the grocery store. Family dinner tonight at five thirty—Dad's cooking. Don't be late."

Leaning against the counter, I stare at my feet. "Mom, can I ask you something, and do you promise you'll tell me the truth?"

"Sure, sweetie. What is it?"

"Does my hair look stupid?"

She tilts her head, studies my face. "You look fine. It's just . . . you look different than you used to." She hugs me, pecks me on the cheek, and then grabs her car keys and leaves.

14

ALPHA DOGS

When I pull up to the skate park Taj and Ricky sit on the hood of Taj's car, listening to music. "Hey, Cinderella. Glad you could make it." Ricky nods in my direction, smiling. Taj holds up my board and helmet. "Missing something?" I get out of my car and he hands 'em to me.

"Thanks," I say, grabbing the stuff out of his hands.

"Hey, we remembered your dinner, too," Ricky blurts out.

I look in my helmet—a half-eaten, crusty burger and a bunch of cold french fries are stuffed in there. Taj punches Ricky in the arm and they both start laughing like a couple of yappy hyenas.

We head into the park. Skeeter emerges from the snack shack, his scraggly hair pulled back into a thin string of a ponytail. He raises his hand upward and gives me a high five. "Josh, dude . . . long time no see." He gestures with his head, nodding toward Taj and Ricky. "This your new crew?"

"Yeah. These are my friends Taj and Ricky."

"Taj Roberts and Ricky Ro Ro Rodriguez. I know who these guys are," Skeeter bellows. "Hey . . . you guys got any posters you could autograph?" He looks around, rubbing his hands together. "You know, not for me. The groms around here really go in for that sort of thing."

Ricky shakes his head. "Nah, dude, not today." He clenches his jaw, gazing at the street course.

"We're just here to skate," Taj pipes in, a skateboard dangling from his hand.

"Yeah, okay. Some other time." Skeeter holds out his hand for a fist bump.

Both Taj and Ricky drop their boards on the pavement and roll into the park. I look at Skeeter and shrug. "Sorry, dude," I say and give him another high five. "Take it easy." I plop my board on the ground and skate away.

When I catch up with Taj and Ricky, they're both standing at the top of the vert ramp. Taj is set up on the coping. "This ramp is *so* sick," he says. "Dude, you're stoked." He stomps on the front of his board and swooshes into the ramp, busting a fat air out the other side. He takes a nice long run, and then Ricky goes for it a bunch of times too. I take a couple of turns, but the truth is, I'm not in the mood to skate, so mostly I sit on my board on the top deck of the vert ramp and watch Taj and Ricky session.

After a while we head over to the street course. When Taj and Ricky see the setup they're like a couple of little kids at Disneyland. They air over stairs, their boards spinning underneath them. They tailslide and grind forever along buttery rails. Soon word spreads that the pros are in the park. Skaters stop what they're doing and come over to watch. Kids come up to us, bugging us for autographs, but Taj and Ricky ignore them and keep skating.

I sit there watching when I feel a tap on my shoulder.

"Hey, Josh, where you been?"

"Oh, hey, Cody," I say.

"Your mom tell you I called?"

"Yeah, I've been busy."

"Yeah, me too."

"But maybe next weekend we'll skate," I say.

"Yeah, okay." He nods.

"Hey, Lowman," Ricky calls from the street course. "We're starving. Let's get some food."

I stand up and grab my board, and it's super awkward. "I'll see you around," I say to Cody.

On my way out of the skate park, someone grabs my shoulders from behind and spins me around. It's Big Chad. He wraps his arms around me in a bear hug and picks me up off the ground. "Dude, I haven't seen you since your birthday party." He sets me down and brushes my shoulders off. "Remember when that scumbag stole your board at the contest and you had to use mine? That was *epic*."

"Totally," I say bumping his fist and laughing.

Big Chad points to the board dangling from my hand. He grabs it, flips it over, and checks out the trucks. "No way, this thing is *rad*. Mind if I try it?"

I sigh. "Dude, I can't. I'm sorry. I gotta go."

"Come on, just one quick run," Big Chad pleads.

"They're waiting for me." I point to Taj and Ricky, walking to the car. "Seriously, I'm sorry. Some other time." I pluck my board out of Big Chad's hands and head toward the exit.

Me, Taj, and Ricky hop into my car and head over to Federico's.

We order up a bunch of tacos and sit at a table to wait for our food. Taj pumps the straw up and down in his giant cup of soda, an annoying squeaking sound polluting the room. "So, who's Erin anyway?" Finally he stops making that sound with his straw and takes a drink.

I shrug. "Some girl . . . used to be my friend."

Taj stops drinking. "Not your girlfriend, is she?"

I shake my head. "Nah."

"Well, she better not be."

"Taj is right, dude. Girlfriends are lame," Ricky says.

Our names are called. Ricky pops out of the booth, grabs our tray of food, and delivers it back to the table.

"Why?" I ask.

Taj sets down his food. "Dude, are you kidding me? You're a pro skater. You can get a ton of girls. Any girl you want. You don't wanna be tied down with *one* girl."

Ricky nods, grinning. A piece of shredded lettuce hangs from his lip. "Lots of hookups. Catch and release," he says, his eyebrows undulating up and down on his forehead.

"I'll show you what I mean." Taj points to a girl standing at the counter. "She's cute, right? Watch this." He goes up to her and starts talking. We can't hear what he says, but he points to us and then leads her over to our table. "This is Ricky Rodriguez and Josh Lowman, professional skaters, Alpha Dog Skate Kru team riders." He points out the window toward the curb. "That's Josh's sweet ride. Maybe he'll take you for a spin in it sometime."

Ricky wipes his mouth with a napkin, looks up, and smiles.

"Hi," she gushes.

Taj puts his hands on Ricky's shoulders. "You want Ricky's autograph. It'll be worth some money someday."

Ricky shakes his head. "Come on, dude. You're embarrassing me." He motions to Taj, pretending to write something on his hand. Then he looks back at the girl. "What's your name?"

"Ashley." She looks over at a couple of her friends standing in the doorway, signaling them to wait.

Ricky stares at his food for a second, and then he looks the girl right in the eyes. "Well," he says, "I guess I'd give *you* an autograph, but only if you give me your phone number."

The girl nods. "Okay."

Out of nowhere, Taj magically appears with two napkins and two pens. Ricky takes a napkin, scribbles her name, and then writes something underneath. He signs it and hands it to her. She takes a napkin, writes down her number, and hands it to him, just like that. She waves good-bye, and then dashes out the door to catch up with her friends.

Taj sits back down in the booth, grinning. "See how easy it is? You don't *need* a girlfriend. You can have *any* girl you want." He grabs a taco, chows it down, and slurps up the last of his drink.

But what if you don't want any *girl?* I wanna say. *What if the only girl you want thinks you're the wrong guy, slams the door in your face, thinks your hair is lame?* But I don't say anything. I stare at all the different initials carved into the dull-orange table and then Ricky leans his elbows on the table and starts talking. "See, the thing with you, Lowman, is you just haven't gotten used to it yet. You're one of us now, an alpha dog, but you still think you're like one of those guys back at the skate park, and you're not. You're an *Alpha Dog team rider*, dude, *a VIP*. You just have to start acting like one." He takes the napkin with the girl's phone number on it, scrunches it up into a ball, and throws it in the trash. He pats my shoulder. "Forget this Erin chick."

I listen to his words, let them sink in slowly, and then I stand up. "Let's get outta here," I say. "Let's go skate." We leave our trash on the table and bail.

15

INVISIBLE

At school, when I pass Erin in the hall she's talking to one of her teammates. I try to get her attention, and I know she sees me, but she doesn't look over in my direction. When I sit at the lunch tables with Niko and Cody they barely say three words. I eat my sandwich and it's so quiet, I can hear myself chew. It goes on like this, Monday, Tuesday, Wednesday—the same deal. Erin won't look at me, and Cody and Niko pretend I don't exist.

I figure if they don't want to talk to me, I don't need to talk to them. I quit waiting outside Erin's classes after the bell rings and I don't try to talk to her in the hall. At lunch, I cruise through the lunch area and walk right past Cody and Niko's table. At first, Carl Hansen, a big football player, tries to get me to sit at the jock table, but I don't buy it. They only want me to sit with them now because I'm sponsored and they want free stuff. So what I do is, I sit next to Edgar Glunk and his crew.

Edgar and his pals ramble on about *Star Wars* and some old show they've been watching called *Battlestar Galactica*, and I eat my lunch in peace. My days are filled with avoiding my friends at school, getting caught up on the sickest battle scenes of science fiction, skating at the TF with Taj and Ricky until after dark, getting home, doing my homework, and going to bed. School, skate, homework, sleep. There's no time for anything else, which is fine with me, because *I* am preparing for battle.

The morning of the Godzilla Vert competition, I wake up early, waves of jitters rolling through my gut. I lie in bed staring at the ceiling, fidgeting with the sheets at the foot of my bed. The only thing I can think of to settle my nerves is to do that thing that Zander taught me—I watch myself skateboard in my head like I'm watching a movie. I watch myself drop into the vert ramp, draw a clean line through the bottom and up the next wall, shoot out of the ramp—flying, spinning, landing. I even remember Zander's words—*show up and stick around*. I lie there watching myself skate on my eyelids, repeating Zander's words over and over, but then my mind drifts and the next thing I know, I'm thinking about Erin. I open my eyes, hop out of bed, get dressed, grab my stuff, and go downstairs.

I walk into the kitchen. My dad sits at the counter drinking a cup of coffee and reading the newspaper. He looks up. "Big day today. Want some breakfast?" he asks.

"Nah—not hungry." I lay my hand on my stomach.

"Ah. Pre-competition nerves. Don't worry. You're gonna to do great."

He takes a sip of coffee and rifles through the sections of the *Green Valley Times*. "Hey, Josh, did you see this?" He points to the front-page article in the sports section. There's a picture of Erin's soccer team. They're huddled around in a big circle, their arms hooked across each other's backs, leaping, their ponytails suspended in the air behind them. "Says right here that the VVHS girls' soccer team is having a breakout season. They're playing tonight under the lights at Valley View High," my dad says, reading aloud.

"Cool," I say and head for the door.

When I get to the training facility, a huge van with a big GRUEL TV logo scrawled across the side is parked at the side entrance. A huge inflatable can of Godzilla sports drink sits next to the main entrance, and staff and crew members scurry around like swarms of focused ants. I slide into the building, head straight for the board room, and bang on the door. After a few seconds Steely pops his head out like a Whac-A-Mole trying to avoid the hammer. He shoos me in. "It's a madhouse out there. I'm tellin' you. A three-ring circus," he says. "Come in. Come in before they find us." He closes the door, locking it once we're both inside. He takes a deep breath and looks me up and down. "Big day for you, kid." He glances at the clock. "We got just enough time. Follow me. I wanna show you something." He marches to the back of the board room, motioning for me to follow.

"Ever seen one a these?" Steely points a thumb toward a strange metal contraption resting on a table in the middle of the floor. "Reel-to-reel projector—how we used to watch film in the old days." He grabs two giant wheel-looking things. "Found these the other day buried in a supply cabinet." He pins the wheels to the side of the machine, runs a strip of plastic through a loop, and pushes a button. "Hit the lights, would you?" he says. I flip the light switch and sit cross-legged on the floor. The steady rhythm of the wheels spinning on the projector fills the room, and old footage of vert skating pioneers magically appears on the white sheet Steely pinned to the wall.

Me and Steely sit together in the dark, staring quietly at the movie screen sheet hanging in front of us, and I hear Steely laugh to himself when a couple of gangly dudes make clown faces at the camera. They're wearing corduroy shorts with big front pockets and striped tube socks that go up to their knees. One guy's wearing a pair of deck shoes, the other a pair of high-top sneakers. They don't have their shirts on. They stand at the edge of an empty, kidney-bean-shaped swimming pool looking down into the deep end. A guy with a wild mane of bleached-blond hair and a mouth full of crooked teeth points at his skateboard, gives a thumbs-up, and then drops into the pool. He pops out on the edge. His buddy comes over and throws an arm around him. They both stare into the camera laughing, and it takes a little while until I figure out that I recognize the blond guy's face. "Hey, Steely," I say. "That's you."

Steely chuckles deep from the base of his throat. "That's me and Tommy Sims. Those backyard pools—those were some *good* times," he says.

Then Tommy and Steely and a couple of sunburned teenagers take turns riding the pool, and they have the most beautiful style I've ever seen anyone have on a skateboard. They crouch down low, push their knees forward, extend their arms, and carve the curves of the pool like it's a concrete wave. One guy's about to drop in when the camera flips around 180 degrees and an old man in a wide-collared shirt and high-water polyester pants comes into focus. He's pointing a finger at the camera and screaming. The movie gets all blurry for a second, then refocuses on skaters grabbing their boards, hopping over a wall, and scrambling in five different directions, the camera shaking and bouncing as the cameraman runs away.

The plastic strip of film running through the dinosaur projector pops off the reel and makes a fwapping sound as it spins around and around. Steely turns the projector off, turns on the lights, shaking his head and laughing to himself. He sits back down in his fold-up aluminum chair.

"That was *incredible*," I say.

Smiling, he gets up, starts fiddling with the movie reels, then comes over and sits back down. He takes a deep breath and exhales. "Look, kid," he says, wagging a finger toward the temporary movie screen. "You wanna know why I showed you this?"

I nod.

"It's gonna be a big deal out there today. You're running with the big dogs now. Understand?"

I nod, staring down at the floor.

"Got pros coming up from San Diego, a few boys coming down from LA. Guys coming from all over the place—Oregon, East Coast, Florida. This Godzilla series is a big deal."

I look up. "You think I'm ready?"

"I *know* you're ready." He glances over at the poster of himself when he was younger. "I just wantcha to know that sometimes, things don't turn out the way you think they're gonna." He looks at me right in the eyes. "I just wantcha to know, no matter what, you worked really hard these past few months. You gotten a lot better since we first started working together. That's what matters. So when you skate today, enjoy it. You see what I'm sayin'? Enjoy the moment. That's what I wantcha to remember."

I smile. "You're not getting mushy on me, are you, Steely?"

"Nah." He shakes his head. "I don't even like you."

He stands up, motions me toward the door. "You better get

out there. They're gonna want to talk to you. Rumor's spread that you can pull the nine."

I walk toward the door.

"Don't forget what it's all about now," he says.

"Control and timing?"

"No . . . women!" he snorts, and then cruises back into the board room cracking up at his own joke.

As soon as I walk onto the training facility floor, a guy wearing a GRUEL TV shirt comes up to me and shoves a microphone in my face. Some dude with a giant camera on his shoulder trails after us while the dude with the microphone rattles off a ton of questions. "Hey, Josh, word on the street is you can pull a nine hundred. You gonna go for it today? How do you feel, a first-timer skating with the pros? Are you nervous? Feel ready?"

"Uh, can't talk right now. Gotta warm up." I walk away as fast as I can because as soon as he waves that microphone in my face and asks all those questions, my stomach seizes up and my hands feel clammy.

"After you skate then. We want to talk to you after you skate," Microphone Dude shouts after me as I walk to the competitors' area. Inside the competitors' tent, pros stand around, chatting with one another, telling jokes, laughing—totally calm and relaxed. I almost ask one of them to sign the deck of my skateboard, but then I remember—*I'm here to compete too*—and all of the sudden I can feel sweat beads popping up on my nose. Finally I see Taj and Ricky out of the corner of my eye and I walk over to them.

"Lowman, dude, waz up?" Ricky smiles big and gives me a high five.

Taj walks up behind me and squeezes my shoulder. "What's up, bro?"

"Taj . . . Ricky . . . come find us when you're done," someone shouts from outside the competitors' tent. A huge posse of people head toward the bleachers waving thumbs-up and peace signs to Ricky and Taj as they walk away.

"Who are they?' I ask.

Taj shrugs. "Family . . . friends."

"Where your people, Lowman?" Ricky asks.

I peer into the seating area, finally spotting my mom, dad, and little brother. They see me too and pop to their feet waving. "Right there," I say, waving back.

A few skaters ride the ramp before the competition begins. Every time a pro drops in, cameras click from the stands, and little explosions of light flash like fireflies. I walk over to the competitors' table to see when I skate. They put me last, fifteen guys ahead of me. We each get three turns in the first round and they take our highest score. A loud voice bellows through the arena. It's time to begin. I take a deep breath, exhale, and wander over to where all the other pros are hanging out, waiting for their turn.

Steely wanders over to where I'm standing and we both watch the first five skaters do their thing. They're absolutely amazing—fluid and strong, like they were born with a skateboard attached to their feet. Steely, his hands buried in his pockets, turns to me. "You remember what we been practicing," he says. "On your first run, you go for the nine. If you fall, you got two more chances. On the second run, go for it again." Steely, super intense, lowers his voice. "If you don't land the nine on the second run, don't *worry* about it. But whatever you do, *don't* try a nine hundred on the third run. Forget about that trick and do what you gotta do to make it to the next round." I nod, eyes fixed on the concrete floor in front of me.

Steely grabs my shoulders with his massive hands. "This is it, kid. Now go up there and have some fun." He nods toward the top of the ramp, winks at me, spins on his heels, and takes his seat in the front row next to Dirk Davies.

I'm too wound up to watch the rest of the guys ahead of me skate, so I hang out under the vert ramp for little while until it gets closer to my turn. When there are four guys ahead of me, I put one foot on the first step leading to the top platform and go over the order of my tricks in my head. I can hear the sound of skateboard wheels clunking against the ramp every time a skater lands a trick, and loud cheers of pumped-up fans blast through the arena. I climb more stairs, touch my toes, and rotate my ankles, the vibration of the ramp trembling below my feet every time a skater drops in from the top. With two guys left, I climb a couple more steps. Finally a deep voice booms over loudspeakers, "And new to the arena, ladies and gentleman, Josh Lowman, Alpha Dog Skate Kru team rider."

I step onto the platform, look into the stands below, and I feel like I'm in one of those silent movies. The crowd gazes up at me. I see Steely leaning forward in his chair, his elbow planted against his knee, his chin resting on the palm of his hand, and my mom, dad, and little brother are waving at me from their seats in the middle row. People rock back and forth in gentle waves across the floor of the warehouse, lots of movement, but not too much sound. I set my back wheels against the coping, look across to the opposing wall, eyeballing the exact spot I'm going to hit when I bust out the nine. Then I stomp on the front of my board and charge into the ramp.

For my first few tricks, I spin a smooth 360, land a graceful 540 spin, and nail a stylish frontside tuck knee air. Then I set up for the nine. Pumping the transition nice and hard, I generate a *ton* of speed, twist my torso halfway back, boost super high, and snap my shoulders around the instant I leave the surface. I'm up in the air, spinning—once, twice, a half rotation more. It's blurry. I can't spot the landing, but I know it's down there somewhere. I clunk into the ramp right after completing two and a half rotations, and with the momentum of my board going straight and my body still spinning, I lose my balance and come off my board. "Ohhhhhh-hhhh"—I hear the collective gasp from the crowd fill the arena as I slide across the bottom of the ramp and come to a stop.

I grab my board and try it again and the same thing happens. I just can't get my spins completed fast enough so I land back in the ramp with my body going one direction, and my board going another. On the third run, I do exactly what Steely tells me. I go with spin tricks I know I can land, some cool grabs, some flip tricks on the lip, and I score high enough to squeak into the semifinal.

Me and Ricky battle hard against three other skaters in the semis. I keep trying to land the 900 but *every time*, I keep coming off my board. Ricky sticks to what he's good at. He's all about impossible flip tricks on the edges of vertical walls and he's a *maniac*. I'm pretty sure the final's gonna be between Ricky and this Southland pro who keeps landing crazy tricks, but on my last qualifying run I dig deep and land a kickflip melon 540. *Unbelievable.* Ricky nabs first place, I get second, and both of us advance to the final round.

They give us a fifteen-minute intermission before we start up again. Footage of BMXers soaring through the air and skaters blasting out of vert ramps rolls across a giant screen to keep the fans happy and in their seats. I can hear the chatter of spectators swirling around the arena, and I know what they're waiting for. They want the 9. I'm just not sure that I'm the guy who can give it to them. Out of the hordes of people, Steely emerges, walking toward me, rocking back and forth as he enters the designated competitors-only section. He motions for me to follow him back to the board room. We sneak inside and he shuts the door behind us.

He looks at me, nodding slowly. "How you feelin'?" he asks.

I shake my head. "I don't know what's wrong with me, Steely. I just . . . I can't do it with all those people out there watching me."

"Look, kid," he says. "You know you gotta go for it . . . you gotta go for the nine." He rests his chin in the cup of his hand, rubs his index finger back and forth across his stubbly cheek, studying my face.

I gesture toward the door. "The whole world's out there watching me fall over and over again. Do you have *any* idea what that's like?"

"Yeah, I do. I know exactly what that's like." He stares at me like he's trying to make me understand what he means with his eyes. Then, slowly, he begins to speak. "Doesn't matter who's watching," he says, "'cause I know you can do it, and you know you can do it. You don't pull it, you get second place. You pull it . . . you make history. You ain't got nothin' to lose."

"All those people," I mutter.

"Forget about 'em. They don't know you . . . *I* know you."

"I just . . . There's too many people. I can't do it."

"Forget about 'em. All those people. Pretend they're invisible. Pretend it's you and me up there, no one else. And then just skate, just like you do all the time."

The announcer's voice vibrates through the walls of the board room: "Josh Lowman, where are you? We're ready to start."

I stare at the floor, shaking my head. Steely squeezes my shoulder. "Come on," he says, "it's time."

He opens the door, leads me down the hallway, and marches me through the crowd. When we get to the bottom of the vert ramp, he looks me in the eyes, then turns around and takes his seat.

I climb the steps up to the top, my board dangling at my side. Ricky comes over, gives me a high five, turns and waves to the crowd. He walks over to the edge of the ramp, gets set up, and waits for the clock to start running. He busts out a series of *phenomenal* tricks, his skating smooth and fluid. He pops out of the ramp at the end of his run, stretches his arms out toward the bleachers, and pumps his fist in the air, smiling as people cheer. He grabs me by the arm, whispers in my ear, "Pull that nine, Lowman . . . I *know* you can do it—go for it!" He pats me on the back, looks out to the crowd, points to me, and then holds nine fingers up in the air. And they start chanting "Nine, nine, nine."

I take a deep breath and look toward Steely. He closes his eyes, drops his chin to his chest, and puts his fingers in his ears. He pops his head back up, points at me, then taps his chest, slowly mouthing the words, *You and me.* He closes his eyes, drops his head, and puts his fingers in his ears again. I set my board up on the coping, hold it in place with my back foot, and then do the same as Steely. I close my eyes, use my fingers as earplugs, and try to remember what it feels like to land on the ramp after spinning two and a half rotations. I'm not sure that I can do it, but when I open my eyes and unplug my ears, hear the crowd chanting, see the number 9 flashing across the big screen, I know that I have to try.

The clock starts running. I drop in. I go with frontside airs, throwing in a few different grabs—work on getting my legs warmed up and ready. And with ten seconds left on the clock, I pump through the bottom of the ramp, generating as much speed as I can. *This is it. Do or die.* I crank my shoulders back, suck my knees into my chest, air out of the ramp, and use my entire torso to throw my arms around. I'm spinning, up in the air spinning fast, once, twice, half a rotation more. I spot the landing. Complete silence, except for the clunk of my wheels smacking back into the ramp. Using my arms like windmills for balance, I try my hardest to stay on my board. I bend my knees into a deep squat, my back hand almost grazing the floor, and I hang on, hang on for dear life. I use every muscle in my body, my legs, my stomach, my shoulders to force my feet to stick to the deck of my skateboard and I ride it out. I *land* the 900 and roll away.

The crowd goes *ballistic.* Cameras click, lights flash. People jump out of their seats, give each other high fives, hug, laugh, scream, and cheer. Programs float through the arena like confetti. Images of me spinning, almost falling, pulling the landing flash across the giant screen, and then the slow-motion replay cuts to live footage of people dancing in the aisles. I'm standing there in a daze, then Ricky runs up, takes my fist, pushes it straight up into the air, and the crowd goes wild.

The Gruel TV dude shows up, wraps his arm around my shoulder, and pulls me in tight. "Josh, you're the first skater to ever pull a nine hundred in competition. You're going down in the history books. Right now, in this moment, how do you feel?" I look into the crowd, try to find my family, look for Steely, search for a familiar face, but I can't find anyone that I recognize. "It feels . . . good," I say, my voice amplified through the microphone.

Dirk and Steely appear out of nowhere. Dirk puts his arm around me, beams into the camera, and starts talking about the dominance of Alpha Dog team riders. Using his thick body to create a pocket of calm, Steely pulls me aside. He rests both his hands on my shoulders, locks his eyes on mine, and we stand together for a couple of quiet seconds. He takes a step back, his blue eyes glowing, points a thick finger at my chest, and without saying a word he turns around and disappears into the crowd.

I hear a voice I recognize call my name. When I turn around, Mikey runs over and leaps into my arms. My mom hugs me. "Josh," she says. "I had no idea." My dad hugs me too. "*Great job,*" he says.

The president of Godzilla sports drinks, Dirk, Taj, and Ricky walk over to where me and my family are standing. They hand me a giant gold trophy. My parents and my brother stand off to the side while we pose for a bunch of pictures. When we're finally through, Dirk loosens his tie. "Party at my house tonight," he says. "You're all invited. We have a lot to celebrate." He and the Godzilla president turn and head toward Dirk's office. Ricky looks at me, grinning. Taj nods, mouthing the words, *Lots of girls,* his eyebrows dancing up and down on his forehead.

People I don't know approach me from every direction. "Josh, we'd like to talk to you about a sponsorship," "Is your contract with ADSK exclusive?" "We want you to wear our shoes." They circle me like sharks in a feeding frenzy shoving cards into my hand. My mom and dad come to my rescue, one on each arm. Mikey grabs my hand and they guide me through the fray. We get to a hallway. There are no people and it's quiet. I lean against a wall, take a deep breath, and close my eyes—glad it's finally over. Then we head for the exit.

"You want to go to Dirk's party, you can, sweetie," my mom says. "Just be home by curfew."

I play with the buckle on my helmet, snap it in and out. "Don't feel like it," I say.

"Wanna come and grab a bite to eat with us?" my dad asks.

"Nah." I shake my head.

My mom squeezes my arm. "Well, what are you going to do then, honey?"

"Go watch Erin's soccer game," I say.

My dad puts his arm around my shoulder and they walk me out to my car.

I drive toward Green Valley, hoping I'm not too late. When I pull into the parking lot of Valley View High, the soccer field's glowing under the stadium lights. I hustle across the parking lot. Luckily, I get there just in time to see the last fifteen minutes of the game. Bright-orange numbers light up the scoreboard at the far end of the stadium. Erin's team is winning by one. There's hardly anyone in the stands watching, mostly moms and dads and a few faces I recognize from school. I take a seat on a far bench in the corner by myself.

I spot Erin. She's chasing a free ball across the field and she's fast. Her ponytail bounces up and down when she runs. She pumps her arms and moves her feet, black-and-white cleats racing across green turf. She gets to the ball and blasts it downfield. She doesn't stop moving, doesn't stop to celebrate. She slows down a little but stays completely focused on where the ball is, where it's going.

Finally the clock runs out. Every girl on Erin's team runs to the middle of the field, laughing, hugging, and leaping in the air. Everyone files onto the field to join in the celebration and I'm left standing in the bleachers alone. A coach pulls Erin aside, starts talking to her, and as she listens she glances up toward the stands. I'm pretty sure she sees me, but then a girl runs up and pulls her back into the circle. She throws her arms around her teammates. There's no lights, no cameras, no crazy crowd. I stand there watching Erin—surrounded by friends—people who like her just because. And she looks happy, really happy—the way you're supposed to look when you win.

16

ALPHA LOYALTY

At school everyone except Erin, Cody, and Niko wants to be my best friend. People I've never talked to before come up to me and shake my hand. At lunch, two linebackers from the football team come over and escort me to their lunch tables. They're big dudes, so I don't argue. I eat my lunch with the football players. The quarterback invites me to a party at his house on Saturday night, and some kid from the school newspaper stops by the table and asks if he can write a feature story about me for the next issue. A bunch of cheerleaders sit down at the table. One of them whips a skateboarding magazine out of her notebook and flips it open to the center page. There's the picture of me, Taj, and Ricky standing next to Dirk's car. She tells me her little brother's really into skating and asks me to sign it.

I never really looked at that picture before. I mean, I saw it in the magazine, but I never really *looked* at it. My hair's cut close to my head. Arms folded across my chest, no smile, jaw set, I gaze into the camera. I glance over to the area where Erin usually sits and look over at Cody and Niko's table too. They're all sitting in their usual spots. The cheerleader hands me a pen. I look at the picture of me, Taj, and Ricky one more time before I sign it—all three of us standing there looking tough, looking alpha, looking like we're standing on top of the world. I sign my name, close the magazine, and hand it back.

After school, I walk into the TF and head to the board room to let Steely know I'm ready to skate, but when I ask him to come over to the ramp with me he clucks his tongue and shakes his head. "Can't skate right now," he says. "Dirk wants to see us in his office."

I tilt my head.

"Dunno what for." Steely shrugs. "Says he wants to see us first thing, that's all."

When we walk into Dirk's office, he spins around in his chair to face us, smiling. He motions for us to sit down in a couple of chairs facing a TV screen. "Afternoon, gentlemen," he says. "Nice work at the Godzilla Vert competition, Josh, Steely." He looks at both of us and nods. "I have a feeling that what we've accomplished together so far is just the beginning. I have a little something I'd like to show you." He presses a button on a remote control, gets up, turns off the lights, and then, sitting down, he leans back in his chair.

Deep drums, the kind they play in orchestras, boom through the TV speakers, and then really dramatic music begins to play above the steady rhythm. An image of a skater flying through the air in slow motion, arcing through blue sky, glides across the screen. Suddenly the music stops, and the sound of skateboard wheels slamming against a ramp echoes through the dark room. The camera pulls back. The Great Wall of China stretches across the screen, and the narrator's deep voice seeps through the speakers: "Danny Way and the development of the mega ramp are pushing the sport of skateboarding into a limitless future."

Dirk hops out of his chair and turns on the lights. "Well, what do you think?" he asks.

"Danny jumping the Great Wall of China. Seen it a million times," Steely grumbles.

"That's not the point." Dirk moves his index finger in the air as he speaks. "That thing the narrator says at the end—that the mega ramp is pushing skateboarding into a *limitless future*. That's the point." He slides his gaze from me to Steely, and then shifts around in his chair. "Look, Danny's bringing the mega ramp to the X Games—it's going to be a game changer, and we need to figure out how to be a part of it."

"Listen, Dirk. I don't mean no disrespect, and I know that you'll be right where the action is," Steely says and rises out of his chair. "But in the meantime, me and the kid here got some skating to do. So if you don't mind we're gonna head out to the floor and get started."

"No." Dirk puts his hand up to stop him from leaving the room. "Sit down . . . let me explain." Pausing for a second, he clears his throat. "Like I said, skateboarding is moving in a new direction, and I see an opportunity here. Now, of course, I want ADSK and myself to be a part of it." He points to Steely, then to me. "And I want you and you to be a part of it too."

"I don't understand what you're gettin' at." Steely folds his arms across his chest.

Dirk puts an elbow on his desk and leans forward. "I got a phone call from Robby Quest this morning. He saw the footage of Josh's nine hundred on Gruel TV."

"Uh-huh." Steely nods.

"Robby has the only permanent mega ramp set up on the West Coast. It's invite-only. He called to invite Josh out. He wants *Josh* to skate it." Dirk swivels his head toward me. "What do you think?"

I pluck my ball cap off my head and brush my hand across my scalp. "I, uh, guess I could try it. As long as Steely would help me," I say.

"Steely will help you all right. He'll train you, right, Steely?"

Steely studies my buzzed hair as I scratch the back of my head, the intensity in his face making me squirm in my seat. "Wait a second. Turn your head that way," he orders, pointing toward the wall. I look to where he's pointing then look back. Steely shakes his head slowly. "Nah. It's no good. Sorry to break this to you, Dirk, but this kid ain't got no business skating the mega ramp," he says.

"What are you talking about? Do you see how much air he gets out of a regular vert ramp? Do you *know* what he could do on a mega ramp?" Dirk's eyes gleam as he talks. "You think a nine hundred's big? I'm talking rotations in the *thousands*."

Steely keeps shaking his head. "I don't like it. Don't like it at all. It's a *bad* idea."

"It's a great idea. A *phenomenal* idea." Dirk, pauses, closes his eyes for a second, and rests his face in his hands. He takes a deep breath and starts again. "Look," he says. "We put Josh on the mega ramp—it's win–win all the way around. He'll be the biggest name in skating; we'll be the top company in the industry. No one will be able to touch us. Don't you see, Steely? . . . We all win."

"Not if he's a vegetable," Steely says.

Dirk looks at me, then at Steely. "What are you talking about?"

"Kid's had a brain injury—a bad one. A *real* bad one. Been in a coma." Steely reaches over and taps the scars on the back of my head. "You can't put him on the mega ramp, Dirk. *It's too dangerous.* Not worth the risk. The kids got too much to lose."

Dirk's quiet, like all the wind has escaped his balloon. He rests his chin on one hand, taps his desk with the other. Taking a deep breath, he exhales loud enough for us to hear. "Look . . . he'll be wearing a helmet of course. We'll be extra careful. We won't take any stupid risks. We'll do everything on the up and up—we'll be *very* careful."

Steely laughs. "You kiddin' me? You ever seen a mega ramp? Stood next to one? It's eight stories tall. *Eight stories.*" Steely points his index finger toward the ceiling. "The kid drops in from *eight stories* up, launches over a *sixty-foot* gap, and shoots up a *twenty-four-foot vertical wall.*" He grabs the edge of Dirk's desk and leans forward. "You can't be *too* careful. Things happen . . . things happen that you can't *control*, Dirk. You know *exactly* what I'm talkin' about."

Dirk looks at Steely, "Nothing's going to happen. He'll be fine."

Steely shakes his head. "Nope. Sorry." he says. "I don't want no part of this. I know you're gonna do what you're gonna do, but me . . . I want no part." He stands up. "Come get me in the board room when you're ready to skate," he says and walks out the door.

Dirk takes a deep breath. We listen to the sound of Steely's footsteps fading as he shuffles farther and farther down the hall. Dirk stares at me. "We can do it without him," he says, flicking his head toward Steely's empty chair. I'm not sure what to do. I sit there, my hands in my pockets, staring at my shoes.

"Look, Josh, you're your own man, right? You make your own decisions. What do you say we go out to Robby's place and you can check out the mega ramp? See it for yourself. If you decide you want to go for it, Robby will teach you everything you need to know. He's one of the best. He'll take care of you. I promise."

I look at the empty chair next to mine. "What about Steely? I mean, he's my coach," I whisper.

"Don't worry about Steely. He'll come around. You'll see."

"I don't know." I sigh.

Dirk leans forward. "Josh, do you like being on this team?"

"Of course." I shift around in my seat.

"Do you like driving a car, getting free clothes? Getting your picture in magazines?"

I nod, but I can't look at him. I keep my eyes focused on the short gray carpet underneath his desk.

"Good." He leans back in his seat. "Because I think you could be one of the best skaters in the world, and I want to help you get there. But if you don't want to, if you want to jump ship, just let me know. There are plenty of other skaters waiting to take your spot on this team. I've been looking pretty closely at that Jagger Michaels kid."

"Jagger Michaels?" I say.

"Yeah, you remember him. You skated against him in the finals at the Green Valley competition."

"I know who he is." I swallow the lump that's been camping in my throat for the past twenty minutes, wipe my hands on my jeans. Jagger Michaels. I remember the smirk on that loser's face when he stole my board and thought he had me beat. I look up slowly. "I'll do it."

Dirk claps his hands together. "That's it. That's what I'm looking for. *Alpha loyalty.*"

"Alpha loyalty," I repeat under my breath.

"And let's keep this between us, okay? I don't want you to tell *anyone*, not even your parents. I want this to be a surprise—send shock waves through the industry. When people find out we have a young ADSK team rider skating mega, this is gonna be huge."

"Believe me, I won't tell my parents."

"Excellent." He swivels around in his chair and grabs something from the tray of his printer. When he turns back to face me, he has a stack of papers in his hand. "Robby Quest sent these over. You need to fill them out. No one touches his ramp without submitting a release form. I'll sign as your witness and then we're all good." He picks up a pen and motions for me to start signing my name, and when I'm done writing my name on the last page, Dirk slides me a piece of paper with directions to Robby Quest's place. "It'll take about half an hour to get there from Green Valley. I'll meet you out there at three o'clock." He picks up the phone on his desk. "See you tomorrow," he says, and points at the door.

17

HUGE

Robby Quest meets us at the entrance to his compound. He swings a heavy metal gate open, motions for us to pass through, and locks it behind us. A yellow dog, tennis ball in mouth, sits in the back of an old pickup truck parked nearby. A grove of avocado trees surrounds the property around Robby's house, and off in the distance the top of the mega ramp juts out from the side of a mountain.

"That's it," I whisper.

"Yep," Robby says, gesturing with his hand toward the truck. "Hop in."

Dirk and I squeeze into the front seat with Robby and we bounce along a dirt road until we reach the bottom of the ramp. I slide out of the truck totally speechless. The mega ramp is enormous, like a ski jump in the Winter Olympics, like a giant mountain that you could ski down if it were covered in snow. I stare at it protruding up into the sky, trying to grasp how it's even possible to skate it. I close my eyes for a second, try to picture myself rolling into the long, steep ramp—try to see myself air over a gap as long as a semi-truck, land on the other side, and then with all that speed shoot into the quarter-pipe, *two stories tall*. I open my eyes and shake my head. "There's no way I'm skating that," I say.

Robby lets his dog out of the back of the truck and sits on the lowered tailgate. "'Course not," he says. "You don't just walk up and drop in from the top. You work up to it. You see that part right there?" He points to the lower third of the ramp. "That's where you spend the first day. You roll in from there, that first platform. It's only forty feet tall and it feeds into a thirty-foot gap. I've seen you skate. You can pull it, no problem."

Dirk points. "And look. There's netting at the bottom of all the gaps between the launch ramps and landing pads to catch you, in case you fall."

"Exactly." Robby reaches around, grabs a ratty tennis ball, and throws it for his dog. "The first day, you practice getting over the gap—you don't even deal with the quarter-pipe. Just clear the gap and slide to your knees."

The dog drops the slimy tennis ball at Robby's feet and sits there panting. Robby hops off the tailgate, grabs the ball, throws it, and wipes his hand on his jeans. "Next, you start from the middle roll-in. That platform's a little higher than the first." He aims his index finger about two-thirds of the way up from the bottom of the ramp. "You roll in there, clear the forty-foot gap, and get used to the quarter-pipe. Just do some mellow airs out of the top. Get a feel for the landing." He grabs a board and a helmet from the back of the truck and slides into his pads. "And then . . . once you've got that wired . . . you're ready," he says, pointing to the very top of the ramp. "Watch . . . I'll show you."

He and Dirk hop into the pickup truck and drive off. After a few minutes pass, Dirk cruises back down the hill, hops out of the truck and Robby's standing on the first platform, shouting down to us, "Check this out." He rolls in, hitting the jump at the bottom. Sailing over the gap, he lands, and then bails his board, drops to his knees, and slides across the smooth surface until he comes to a complete stop. He pops up, grabs his board, and walks to where we're standing. "Piece of cake," he says.

Dirk looks at me. "Totally safe. No problem."

Robby pops his helmet off and holds it in his hands. He turns to face the ramp. "You've got the beginning, intermediate, and black-diamond advanced levels. Start at the beginning and work your way up. That's all there is to it."

I take a deep breath. Exhale. "I can't believe I'm saying this, but the first roll-in spot does look kind of fun."

"Let's get you up there then." Robby walks over to a storage bin under a tree and digs out a bunch of pads—knee pads, elbow pads, special pads for your butt and torso. He tosses them to me. "The trick is, you don't want to have any bare skin exposed. Everything covered up. Trust me. Road rash sucks," he says, brushing his hand across a gnarly scar on his forearm. He looks at Dirk. "His paperwork in order?" he asks.

"You bet. Got it right here." He takes the papers from the inside of his sports jacket and waves them in the air.

Robby looks at me and winks. "Well, then. You're good to go."

I wrestle into the pads, pop on my helmet, and then we hop into Robby's truck and head up the side of the mountain, stopping at the first set of stairs. Me and Robby get out. "Drive the truck back down and we'll see you at the bottom," Robby hollers to Dirk as we walk up to the first platform. I peer over the edge. Muscles twitching, I stare down from the perch, three stories above the ground.

"This is the beginning level? You sure?" I ask.

He looks at me, nodding. "This part isn't *that* much different from vert," he says. "No worries."

Robby goes first. I watch him sail down the ramp and launch into the sky. My stomach churns and my skin tingles. I concentrate on Robby's words. "*Not that much different from vert,*" I tell myself over and over again. Finally, I set my board up on the ledge, roll in, and once I'm flying down the giant ramp, instinct takes over. There's no thinking, just reacting, and the next thing I know I'm flying through the air. My board pressed to my feet, I sail across the gap, stick the landing, and slide onto my knees, hooting and pumping my fist in the air until I come to a stop.

I pop to my feet, my heart pounding, adrenaline pulsing through my veins. "That was *insane*," I scream. I snatch my board up into my hand and unbuckle my helmet. "Can I do it again?"

Robby gives me the thumbs-up. We hop into the pickup truck and head back up the mountain. I spend the rest of the afternoon rolling in from the first platform, flying through the air and landing. As the sun sinks behind the foothills, shadows creep onto the surface of the ramp and Robby calls it a day. We pile into the truck and head back. Bouncing along, Robby shouts over the noise, "Well, what do you think?"

"Incredible . . . mind blowing," I holler back, my arm hanging out the open window.

Dirk grins. "I told you Robby would take care of you."

"When can I come back?" I shout.

"Just call me to make sure I'm around. You can come out here and skate whenever you want. I'm stoked to see someone young like you into it."

The very next day I head out to Robby's after school and spend the whole afternoon rolling in from the first and second platforms. Like a dog obsessed with a bone, I don't think about anything else. I go to school, eat lunch with Edgar Glunk or the football players, and skate the mega ramp.

After six days of rolling in from the first and second platforms, I arrive at Robby's with Dirk. We pile into Robby's thrashed pickup and head up to the last set of stairs built alongside the mountain, the advanced level, stopping the truck just below the top platform of *the biggest ramp* in the world. The pit of my stomach burns. Beads of sweat settle along my forehead. I shift around in my seat and fumble with the skate tool that's in my hand.

Robby looks at me, studies my face for a second, and then fixes his gaze on the top of the mega ramp. "Look, Josh," he says. "I get the nervous jitters every time I'm up here, and I've been skating this ramp for a while." He twists the key off. "But there's something about doing things that scare the piss out of you, you know?" He hops out of the truck, grabs his board out of the back, and hands me mine. He knocks on the side of the pickup twice and we watch Dirk scooch into the driver's seat. He turns the engine and motors back down the hill, the tires flinging powdery dust into the atmosphere.

Robby studies me for a second, and I wonder if he knows that my stomach's squirming or if he can tell that I have a tight ball in the base of my throat. I drag in a deep breath and Robby starts talking.

"You're ready to ride this ramp, and there's nothing else like it in the world. It's just you, a skateboard, and speed. *Pure* speed. And then flying . . . being suspended up in the air like that." He motions for me to follow him. "You'll see. Do it once and it gets under your skin." We clomp up the stairs, our boards dangling at our sides.

When we finally reach the top of the structure, I stand at the rail and turn around in a complete circle. We're up so high that you can see for *miles*. A stripe of steel-blue ocean stretches across the horizon to the west. To the east, copper mountains stand out against blue sky, and valleys and fields and winding roads cover the flats below.

Robby motions me to the edge of the ramp. "Okay, so here's the deal," he says. He points with his index finger. "Keep a straight line on the way down and whatever you do, don't try to slow down—you need speed to clear the gap. You don't want to come up short. Trust me. Now, you're gonna be going *fast*, but that's a *good* thing. Go with it. Understand? Embrace the speed."

I take a deep breath.

"When you get to the base down there, right where the vert transitions to horizontal before it curves into the jump, you're gonna feel like you have bricks in your shoes, you know? Like when you're on a roller coaster and you get pressed into your seat—that's what it feels like. All that's normal."

I nod slowly, my jaw clenched, my pulse thumping in my ears. Robby brushes his hair from his forehead, pops his helmet on his head, and tightens the chin strap. "Believe me, I wouldn't let you up here if I didn't know that you could do this. Just chill. I'll go first."

He climbs to the top of the drop-in spot and puts his foot on his board to keep it in place. Staring straight down the steep slope, he plants both feet on his board, rolls forward, and I'm left standing at the top of the mega ramp alone. My heart beats so hard and so fast, I feel like it's going to explode out of my chest. I think about dropping into the mega ramp from the first roll-in spot and the second, sailing across the gap, landing, charging into the quarter-pipe, flying up the vertical wall into the air, soaring. When Robby finishes his ride, I take a deep breath, put both feet on top of my skateboard, and drop in.

I draw a straight line to the bottom and I'm going so fast, I can feel the skin stretching back across my face. I feel the bricks in my shoes, the heaviness in my body as I curve into the flat spot right before I hit the launch ramp and soar into the air. Clearing the gap, I pound onto the landing section, my board secure under my feet, and I fly up the vertical wall of the quarter-pipe. I shoot into the air fifty feet above Planet Earth, suspended up there for a long time, floating, before gravity pulls me back down into the quarter-pipe. My wheels smack against the surface, I stick the landing, bail my board, and slide to my knees.

When I finally come to a stop, I lie on the ramp spread-eagle, staring into the sky. My heart races, every nerve in my body tingles, and waves of relief and adrenaline course through my veins. I'm glad it's over; happy I survived . . . and totally ready to do it again. I hop up. Dirk and Robby applaud, the sound of their clapping hands traveling on a slight breeze and disappearing into the air. I grin and grab my board. I can hear my heartbeat thumping in my ears, and I feel the blood pumping through every cell in my body. I head back over to Robby's pickup ready for another run, but before I toss my board in the back, Robby comes over, grabs my skateboard, and flips it over. He takes a skate tool from his pocket. "So here's the deal," he says, wiggling each of my skateboard trucks with his hand. "You gotta check these bad boys before every ride. Make sure they're not loose." He turns the bolts on each truck less than a quarter of a rotation and hands me back my board. We head back up the mountain and I skate the mega ramp from top to bottom three more times that afternoon before we call it a day.

When the sun starts to dip behind the foothills, we walk out of the compound to our cars. Dirk's glowing. "You know what's next, don't you?" he says.

I shake my head, too wiped out to answer.

"Nine hundreds, ten eighties—who knows how many spins you can bust out of that quarter-pipe? I need to get footage of you skating out here. Release it to Gruel TV as soon as possible. Hope you're ready for this, Josh. It's going to be huge."

"Yep." I sigh. My parents think I've been spending afternoons at the TF jumping on a trampoline. "It'll be huge all right," I say. I throw my gear into the backseat of my car and drive home.

18

THE MOST IMPORTANT WORDS

I pick up the slimy tennis ball and huck it toward the avocado trees. Pearl, Robby's yellow Lab, races after it. The days are getting longer and a spring breeze cools the evening air. I grab my stuff out of the back of Robby's truck and head for the gate, but before I get there I turn to face Robby. "Thanks for letting me hang out and skate," I say. "I know I've been coming around a lot." Pearl saunters over to where we're standing, a thread of dog slobber stuck across her muzzle. Robby crouches down on a knee and scratches her behind the ears. "What I tell you?" he chuckles. He stands up, tosses the ball for Pearl, and she bounds after it through the trees. "The mega ramp gets under your skin."

"Yeah," I say, nodding. "I can't think of anything but that drop." I flick my head toward the giant ramp in the distance. "To tell you the truth, I kind of miss my coach and the TF and all, but all I want to do is ride the mega ramp."

"That's right. You train with Steely."

"You know Steely?"

"You kidding me? Everyone in the industry knows Steely. He's first generation. Godfather of air. Legendary. Probably started skating when wheels were made out of clay." Pearl runs up, drops her slimy dirt-encrusted ball at Robby's feet, and finally collapses into a heap.

"How long have you been skating?" I ask.

"Long time. It's my life. Not a bad way to pay the bills. Especially now that I'm my own sponsor."

"Whaddya mean?"

"I mean that you have to be smart in this business. Sponsors don't care about you. Sponsors care about selling product. I don't deal with sponsors anymore. Been burned too many times. I build ramps. Now I'm my own boss. My own sponsor." He gestures toward the silhouette of the mega ramp rising into the fading sunlight. "In fact, I'm going overseas in a couple of weeks. I'm building a mega ramp in Asia. Can you believe that?"

"That's so cool."

"You want to know the secret? Figure out what is that you love to do and do it. The rest falls into place." He stands up and bumps my fist. "See you around," he says.

I walk away, wiped out from another epic day of skating, and when I pass by the side of Robby's house I see a worn-out soccer ball barely visible in the evening sunlight. I stop for a second, stare at the black-and-white-checkered orb resting on the ground, and then slowly head toward my car. I open the driver's-side door and stretch my hands across the roof. "Hey," I holler toward Robby. "Would it be cool if I brought some friends with me out here sometime?"

He rests a hand on the back of his neck. "Sure," he says. "But not anyone can mess around on this thing." He points his thumb toward the monster ramp jutting into the sky. "No one skates it without my permission first. Cool?"

I nod. "Cool," I say and hop in my car.

I turn the engine and roll out of Robby's compound. I spend the whole drive back to Green Valley thinking about calling Erin, thinking about what I'd say . . . about what *she'd* say. I think about maybe even calling Cody and Niko too, inviting them out to the ramp. As soon as I get home I reach for the phone ready to dial Erin's number, but there's a giant knot ball in my stomach 'cause everything's so weird and messed up and awkward, so I set the phone down and stare at it for a while. I pick the phone up again, tell myself I'm gonna call her, but I don't do it. I can't do it. So I call Taj and Ricky instead. I figure, they're still talking to me and they're pros, so maybe Robby would let them drop in from the easy roll-in. At least then I'd have a couple of friends to skate with.

Saturday afternoon, Taj and Ricky swing by my house. We cruise out to Robby's place, punk music blasting from the speakers of Taj's car. Ricky rests his arm on the front seat and twists around to face me. "Dude, Dirk told me to tell you he's meeting us at the ramp. Bringing a videographer with him," he screams over the music.

Taj slaps his hand on the dashboard, keeping time to the beat. "Alpha Dog world dominance," he bellows, trying to make his voice sound just like Dirk's.

Ricky swivels forward, turns the music down, and then twists back in his seat to face me. "So what's the deal with the mega ramp, Lowman?"

"It's rad." I spin my ball cap around backward. "Totally insane. You just have to start from the lower platforms and work your way up, that's all. You should try it. Robby'd let you."

Taj shakes his head. "There's no way I'm skating that thing," he says, reaching for the knob of the stereo and cranking the volume up as high as it will go. I kick back in my seat, music blaring, my board resting between my knees, and watch the neighborhoods of Green Valley pass by.

When we pull into the compound, Dirk and the photographer are already there. We tumble out of the car and I grab my gear. Dirk walks up to us. "Afternoon, gentlemen." He points toward me with his thumb. "Wait till you see this. He's absolutely killing it." With his eyes like laser beams, he waves his index finger between Taj and Ricky. "You should think about skating mega, too. Alpha dominance," he says, bumping our hands with his fist. Taj makes eye contact with me and Ricky, a grin plastered across his clown face.

We hop into the back of Robby's truck and Dirk drives us to the base of the ramp. Taj and Ricky step out and walk across the flat bottom section. Both turning around in full circles, they stare up the huge slope in front of them; then, turning halfway around, they contemplate the humongous vertical wall of the quarter-pipe.

"Man," Taj says, "I've seen it on TV, but it's a whole 'nother deal when you're standing on it."

Ricky looks at me. "You skate this, Lowman?"

"Yeah." I nod.

"From the top?" Ricky points up the side of the mountain.

"Yeah. Watch." I hop into the beat-up pickup truck and Dirk starts driving. First I drop in from the lowest platform, then the middle one. When I get down to the bottom, I holler, "You guys could pull either one of these drops, easy."

Ricky motions with his head toward the top platform. "Let me see you drop in from up there and I'll think about it," he says.

"Photographer's ready, Josh. We want to get this one on camera," Dirk says, folding his arms across his chest.

I grab my board and we all hop in. Me, Ricky, and Taj drive up the road to the highest platform. Arriving at the top, we bolt up the stairs and look around.

"Holy crap." Taj shakes his head. "This is sketchy."

Ricky just looks over the side of the rail to the ground below.

I stand on the roll-in, set up my board, and hold it in place with my foot. "See you guys down at the bottom," I say. I wait for a second, focus, then plant both feet on my board, lean forward, and drop in.

I race down the long slope, gaining speed by the millisecond. I hit the jump, launch over the gap, land on the other side, and as soon as my wheels smack down something doesn't feel right—I'm going so crazy fast, my board starts to wobble underneath me. Heading straight toward the giant quarter-pipe, I try to gain control. I veer left, try to make my board stop wobbling, but everything's happening so fast, I don't have time to think. My positioning's off, my feet aren't right, but I'm flying toward the vertical wall and there's not much I can do about it. I have to spin backside out of the ramp, losing sight of everything in the blur.

I twist in the air fifty feet above the ground. I can't spot the landing, can't see the ramp below me, but I know it's down there and I'm heading for it fast. At the last second, I see coping. I hit the ramp with most of my weight on my back wheels. My board squirrels out from underneath me and I go down hard—my butt hits first, then my back, shoulders, and then bam, it's quiet and everything goes dark.

When my eyes flutter open, a face hovers above mine. "Josh?

Can you hear me? It's Dirk. You fell. They're taking you to Green Valley Hospital." My eyes float open and close. Then doors click shut and a siren begins to wail.

At the hospital people talk and move in slow motion. All I really want to do is go to sleep, but every time I close my eyes someone taps or pinches me. People I don't know dressed in pale-blue hospital clothes keep asking me questions, asking me to do things. Do you know your name? Do you know what day it is? Can you squeeze my hand, point your toes? It takes me a little while to figure out what they're saying—like they're all swimming underwater.

I feel hands on my arms, hear voices I think I recognize, and when my vision finally steadies, my parents come into focus. My mom bites her lower lip. My dad stands over me, his shoulders hunched. Leaning in, their faces float above mine. "Josh, honey, it's Mom." My dad squeezes my hand. "Josh, it's me, Dad. Can you hear me, son? Can you hear me?"

I try and move my head, but I can't. "Mom, Dad," I mumble. "I'm okay."

They bury their heads in my chest and I can feel their bodies trembling against mine. A doctor comes into the room. I can barely focus, barely comprehend what's going on around me. There's my mom, my dad, a doctor—mouths moving—a string of words. "Spending the night, neurological monitoring, keep our eyes on him." And then the best words—the most important words of all—"He's going to pull through."

19

SECOND CHANCES

After five thousand tests, poking me here and there, looking into my eyes with special cameras, putting me in this machine and that one over there—after five thousand tests, they finally let me do what I've wanted to do since they unloaded me from the ambulance. They let me sleep. I take a short nap and when I open my eyes, my mom and dad are sitting in chairs next to my bed.

"Josh?" my mom says. "Josh, you awake?"

"Yeah," I mutter.

They hop out of their seats and stand next to me. My mom runs her hand across my forehead. "Thank God you're all right, sweetheart."

I look around. Monitors and tubes and beeping machines with blinking, glowing lights fill every corner of the room. My dad, grabbing a pitcher from a shelf, pours me a glass of ice water. "Dirk called. He told us what happened," he says.

"What'd he tell you?" I say, twisting the sheet around my foot at the end of the bed.

My mom plants her hand on my forearm. "That you were skating at the training facility. That you fell. Hit your head against the ramp. Do you remember, Josh?"

"Yeah," I say. "I remember."

They both stand above me, their faces magnified, waiting for an explanation. I take a deep breath and exhale. "I, uh . . . I lost control." My mom and dad are motionless, their heads bowed. All I can hear is their breathing and the sound of the monitor measuring the beats of my heart. "My head really hurts. I don't feel like talking about it right now," I say, and my mom and dad nod slowly and don't ask any more questions.

I turn my head slowly, close my eyes, and take a long, slow drink of water. Every inch of my body aches like I got pummeled by a bus. "Do Cody and Niko know? What about Erin? Does she know?" I say, staring out the window.

My dad pours more water into my glass. "Dirk asked our permission to release a statement on Gruel TV and we agreed. He said he wanted to be out in front, control the story before rumors start spreading. I think a lot of people know."

My mom plops down in a chair next to my bed. She massages her temples, her fingertips rotating in small circles on each side of her forehead. My dad drops into a chair beside her, tilts his head back, and closes his eyes. I look at them, worn out and ground down, like they haven't slept in a million years. "Mom, Dad," I say, "I'm sorry." I open my mouth to speak, to try to tell them the truth about what really happened, but the words get clogged in my throat, and I don't do it. So the three of us hang out in my hospital room, too beat up to do anything else but sit together staring at the walls, until the sound of footsteps moving toward us echoes through the hallway.

A nurse ducks into the room. She peers at her watch and then glances at my parents. "Josh should get some rest," she says.

My parents stand up, both of them stretching slowly. One at a time they lean over and kiss me on the cheek, and then my dad takes my mom by the hand and they leave. There's nothing to do but stare at the clock on the wall and watch time crawl by. Finally, I turn off the lights. Lying in the dark, I listen to the buzzing and humming and chirping of the hospital at night, and when I finally do fall asleep, the night nurse wakes me up every hour to make sure my head's okay.

Early the next morning the usual cast of characters dressed in light-green hospital scrubs parade in and out of my room, taking my blood pressure, listening to my heart, and looking into my eyeballs. I hope that once visiting hours start, maybe Erin or Cody or Niko will stop by, but the only visitors who show are my mom and dad, who walk into my room at 9 AM sharp.

Eventually a hospital attendant dude takes me downstairs in a wheelchair for another round of testing. When I get back to my room, a plate of something covered in clear plastic with a bow on top sits on the counter next to my bed. The nurse pokes her head in the doorway. She points to the gift. "A young lady dropped that at the front desk for you."

"Really?" I ask. "Who was it? What'd she look like?"

"Tall. Wearing soccer shorts. Hair pulled back in a ponytail. Pretty." She flashes me a smile.

I sit up a little taller. "Erin," I whisper to myself. "What'd she say? Did she want to see me?"

"Nope." She shakes her head. "Didn't ask to see you. Just asked us to make sure that you got that gift." She gestures toward the side table, winks, and then darts out of the room practically bumping into my parents, who walk in carrying bags of food.

My dad pushes the plate from Erin over and sets down our lunches. "Where'd you get these?" He fishes a homemade oatmeal cookie off the plate from under the plastic cover and takes a bite. "Um, good."

"Erin," I say.

"She came by to see you," my mom says. "That's nice."

My dad hands me a sandwich. I play with the wrapper and watch my mom and dad eat. My mom looks up from her sandwich, stops chewing, and studies my face. "You all right, honey? Your head hurt?" She sets her food down and sits on the edge of my bed.

"I'm fine," I mutter. "Just not very hungry."

My dad opens a bag of chips and pops one in his mouth. I take a few bites of my lunch, but mostly I lie there staring at the plate of cookies next to my bed.

After a while, Attendant Dude pops into my room again. "Doctor's orders. We gotta go downstairs one more time for a brain scan," he says. "But we'll leave you alone after this round of testing." He helps me into a wheelchair. My dad grabs another cookie, and then my mom and dad walk with us down the hall to the elevator. "We'll be back in a little while," my mom says. They both kiss me gently on the top of my head.

When I get back to my hospital room, late-afternoon sun filters through the window. I lie in bed, and I'm half asleep when I hear a tap on the door. I sit up and I think my eyeballs might be playing tricks on me, so I blink again, trying really hard to focus, because when I look over I can't believe what I see. *Brendon Johnson* is standing in the doorway. I stare at him, not really sure what to say.

He clears his throat. "Um, mind if I come in?"

I shift around in my bed. "Uh, yeah, no. Of course. Come on in." I motion with my hand.

He shuffles across the floor and takes a seat next to me. He looks *so* different from the night me and Erin saw him creeping around the mini mart. Clear eyes peer out from his face, and he's not so skinny anymore.

"I, uh, came by to see how you're doing," he says, tucking his hands into his armpits and leaning forward.

"Head's a little sore," I mutter. "You?"

"I . . . I'm in this program now." He looks up. "It's helping me out a lot."

"That's good." I dig a finger under the hospital ID bracelet on my wrist.

"Starting to skate again, too."

"Great," I say.

Brendon stares at his feet, and I fix my eyes on a blank TV screen because I don't know what else to do. Brendon rubs his hands back and forth across his thighs. "Look," he says finally. "There's something I need to say to you." He stops moving his hands. "I—I'm sorry." He takes a deep breath. Gazing at the ceiling, he closes his eyes. "So, so sorry," he whispers, his voice quivering, and when he opens his eyes again tears stream down his cheeks. "I'm sorry I just stood there that night you got beat up . . . . I'm sorry I didn't come see you in the hospital afterward. Sorry I bailed on you as a friend." He wipes his eyes with the back of his hand. "I'm sorry for everything."

My chin rests on my chest, and I focus on my fingers, interlocked and folded in my lap. Brendon buries his face in his hands. He sobs, his body heaving, and I watch him, tears streaming down my face too. I don't say anything, I just let him cry, and I feel like I'm watching a guy set down a giant load of heavy rocks he's been carrying for a long time.

I wipe tears from my face. "Brendon," I say. "It's okay.". And I mean it. I'm tired of being mad at him. Tired of worrying and wondering about him. Seeing him here, listening to him apologize, I finally set down a heavy rock I've been carrying too. And when he stops crying, and we wipe the tears from our faces, I think we're both a little bit lighter.

He stands up. "I gotta go now. Hope you feel better soon." He heads for the door, but before he leaves he turns around. "Hey," he says. "Can I ask you something?" I nod. "Do you believe in second chances?"

I look him right in the eyes. "Yeah, I do," I say.

He starts to walk away. "Hey Brendon," I call after him. He turns around and faces me. "When I get out of here, let's skate."

"I'd like that. That'd be cool," he says. Turning, he walks out the door, and with the sound of his footsteps echoing and fading through the glowing hallway, he disappears.

20

GRAVITY

After three days of being in the hospital, my doctor sits down with my parents and me. "You're a lucky young man," she says. "This head injury of yours could have been a lot worse. You might not be so lucky next time." I can't stand to look any of them in the eyes, so I stare at my shoes instead. "No driving, no skating, no school for two weeks," the doctor says, and then she signs my release papers and we leave.

I spend the first few days out of the hospital bored out of my mind. I can't watch TV 'cause it makes my eyes hurt and I can't read for too long 'cause it gives me headaches. I'm so bored that I'm actually stoked when my parents announce that Zander's coming over to help me with my homework. At exactly 2:37 PM the doorbell rings. I open the door and there he is. "Josh, my man," Zander says, giving me a high five. "How you feeling?"

"Not so bad," I say and motion for him to follow. I head out the back door to the patio, and we plop down across from each other at the old rickety picnic table in my backyard. I dig into my backpack and fish out a giant textbook. Zander grabs it. "What chapter we on?" he asks. I slide the homework handout from my science teacher in Zander's direction. He flips the book open, starts reading the chapter that covers the laws of gravity, and we sit there soaking up rays in the afternoon sun. Zander's face is in the book and he's reading away. "Gravitation, or gravity, is the force that causes two particles to *pull* toward each other." By the third sentence, I'm totally off in lala land. He looks up. "You following this?"

"Yeah, totally," I lie.

"What'd I just say?"

"Something about gravity."

"Yes." He gives me a thumbs-up. "And gravity is . . . ?"

"Uh, don't know."

Zander rubs his hands together. "Okay, let me try to explain. Gravity's a force, you know? But it's invisible. And it holds things together. It keeps the earth and the other planets in their orbits around the sun and it keeps the moon in its orbit around the earth. So, just like it says right here"—he taps the page with his finger—"gravity is an invisible force that makes two things pull toward each other. Make sense?"

"Kind of." I stare over Zander's shoulder not focusing on anything at all.

Zander closes the book. "You all right? Your head hurt?" He studies my face.

I take a deep breath. "I'm fine," I say.

"No, really. What is it?"

"It's nothin'."

Zander stares at me. "Talk," he says like a Russian intelligence agent, sweeping his index finger across his throat like it's a dagger, "or I vill keel you."

Laughing, I fumble with the pen in my hand.

"But seriously, dude. What's up?" he says.

I watch a plane crawl through the sky in the distance, take a deep breath, and blow out all the oxygen from my lungs. "It's nothin'," I say. "I'm fine." I clench my jaw and stare at the tabletop in front of me.

Zander arches an eyebrow. He lays his arms across his chest and stares me down until I can't take it anymore. "Okay," I say, shifting around in my seat a little. "The thing is." I rub my hands back and forth along my pant legs. I take a deep breath and exhale. "See, the thing is, here I am an *Alpha Dog team rider*, right? And I got *all* the clothes and my picture in the magazines and a sick car sittin' in my driveway." I gesture toward the front yard. "See, *that's* the problem," I say. "I have *everything* every skater in the world *dreams* of, but . . . never mind."

"No. Go ahead. Say it."

I sigh. "My old friends don't want to talk to me and my new friends—I'm not even sure they *are* my friends. And before I got hurt, *all* I did was skate. I didn't have time for *anything* else and I thought I'd love it, but . . . it's just that . . . it's not the way I thought it was gonna be."

Zander shrugs. "So, quit."

I look at him, my head tilted. He fixes his eyes on mine. "If you're not happy, then quit ADSK," he says.

"Quit? I can't *quit*. What would people think?"

"Who *cares*?" Zander locks his fingers together and cradles the back of his head. "Quit the team and keep skating. Just like before. You gave it a shot and now it's time to move on. Simple."

He picks up the textbook, finishes reading, and then talks me through the questions at the end of the chapter, writing down what I say. When we're finished, he stands up. "Look," he says. "You don't need your picture in magazines, or free clothes, or a cool car. It's about you and a skateboard. That hasn't changed. Remember that." We walk through my house to the front door.

"Hey, Zander." He lets go of the doorknob and faces me. "Thanks," I say.

He smiles. "See you tomorrow."

After Zander leaves I go hang out in my room. I stare at all the ADSK posters on the walls and then I get down on my hands and knees, fish around under my bed, and pull out an old poster—the one of Danny Way airing over the Great Wall of China. I study it for a while and then pull out my old clothes and throw on one of my favorite old T-shirts. I reach deep under the bed frame and pull out one of my old ball caps when my hand catches on a notebook from first semester, and it slides out from underneath my bed.

Sitting cross-legged on the carpet, I open the notebook and peer inside. That essay that I wrote about *The Catcher in the Rye* rests in the inside pocket, and the outline that Erin helped me write is on the first page. I read the notes, look at the pictures Erin doodled on the side of the page, tracing over her words with my hand. Then I read some of the stuff I wrote—*My advice to Holden Caulfield: If he wants to have real friends, he has to quit being a jerk and a phony. He needs to figure out who he is and quit worrying so much about what other people think. And one more thing—he needs to man up, call Jane Gallagher, and tell her how he feels.*

I read those lines over and over. I slap my old ball cap on my head, roll the essay up, shove it in my back pocket, and head for the front door. "Going for a walk," I holler.

"Be home in time for dinner," my mom shouts back.

I walk six straight blocks to Erin's house. Her parents' cars aren't in the driveway and I'm not sure if anyone's home, but I stand at her front door and knock anyway. When she answers, she doesn't say a word, she just stands there looking at the ground. I look at her, tears welling up in my eyes, hands in my pockets. "I'm sorry," I say. "I'm sorry for being such a jerk."

When she finally looks up, tears are rolling down her cheeks too. "I missed you," she says. She opens her arms and I walk into them and we stand there in her doorway crying. Gravity is an invisible force that pulls two things together. I stand there holding Erin Campbell and I never want to let go.

21

CHOICES

My mom and dad sit in our living room eating grilled cheese sandwiches and watching the news. "Mom? Dad?" I say. "Can I talk to you for a second?"

My dad grabs the remote and taps the PAUSE button. "Sure. What's up?" he says.

"Well, I've had something on my mind lately." I stare at my shoes. "I was thinking . . . I was thinking that instead of sitting around the house all day long while everyone else is at school and work, I was thinking that maybe I could take the bus out to the training facility?"

My mom looks at my dad and sets down her sandwich. She studies my face before she speaks. "Josh, you heard what the doctor said, right?"

I nod.

"You have to be really, *really* careful," she says.

My dad takes a drink of his iced tea, sets it down on the side table next to him. "Yep. *Really* careful. You're not out of the woods yet."

"I know I'm not . . . and I, I'm really sorry for everything I've put you guys through." The back of my throat kind of burns and

I can feel a knot clenching in my stomach.

"We'll give you permission to go to the training facility on one condition." My mom looks at my dad and nods slowly. "*No skating*," my dad says.

"Deal." I swivel around on my heels and head up to my room.

In the morning I walk through our neighborhood to the bus stop when I see Mrs. Thompson's car parked on the street with a bright-orange FOR SALE sign taped to the side window. I peak inside. Burgundy-red bench seats stretch across the interior. The steering wheel is huge with a sick gearshift jutting from the steering column. I take a step back. Four doors, clean tires, a few dents here and there, but nothing major—someone's gonna be super stoked to get their hands on Mrs. Thompson's sweet car. I look at my watch and then hustle down the sidewalk so I don't miss the bus.

When I finally get to the TF I walk straight through the doors to the board room. I hear Steely rustling around as I knock.

"Come in," he grumbles.

He looks up, sees that it's me, and sets down what he's doing. "Kid. I sure am glad to see you," he says. "You all right?"

I nod. "I'm okay. Came by to see if I could help you out around here."

A tower of unopened boxes rests in the center of the room. "Think I could find something for you to do." He tosses me a box cutter. "How 'bout we start right here?"

We work together for a long time, quietly sliding razor blades through cardboard and making stacks of skate decks across the board room floor. I'm stomping on piles of empty containers, and then I stop what I'm doing and look over in Steely's direction. "Did you see it?" I say. "Did you see my fall?"

Slicing through the top end of a cardboard box, he peers into the opening. "Saw it. Dirk showed me the footage."

"What the heck happened?" I pick up a brand-new skate deck, not a scratch, ding, or chip on it, and flip it around in my hands. "I mean I *made* that drop, *pulled* the landing a bunch of times."

Steely puts down his box cutter. He looks at me for a few seconds. "You got speed wobbles. You overcorrected."

"I didn't know what else to do. I was going fast . . . *uncontrollably* fast . . . and then I was heading straight for the quarter-pipe."

He shakes his head. "You got lost up there." He points toward the ceiling. "Wait here," he says. He dips into his office, then comes back holding my skateboard. "This is the board you was ridin'. You weren't paying attention." He flips it over, moves the trucks from side to side. "You can't drop in on a ramp like that with trucks like this." He takes a skate tool out of his back pocket, twists the bolt on each truck a quarter of a degree, and hands me my board. "Here you go."

I stare at it in my hands, swallow hard thinking about hurtling down the mega ramp, my board wobbling uncontrollably underneath me, the quarter-pipe waiting to hammer me. My whole body tightens. "It wasn't just the trucks," I whisper. "I should've *never* let Dirk talk me into riding the mega ramp in the first place."

Steely makes a clucking sound with his tongue. "Nah. Sorry, kid. This ain't Dirk's fault."

"You should have heard him. He threatened to kick me off the team."

"Look," Steely says, shaking his head. "I know it makes you feel better thinking you had nothin' to do with this." He slides his skate tool into his back pocket. "Believe me. I spent a lot of time blaming other people for my problems. It almost killed me," he whispers.

I look at him. He points to the GODFATHER OF AIR poster on the wall and then clears his throat. "A long time ago, I got caught up in the whole pro skater thing. Did an impossible trick—something I had *no* business doing. Didn't make the landing. Crashed into the deep end. Broke my back. Doctors said I'd never skate or walk again. Luckily they was only right about one of those two things."

"You *never* skated again?"

"Can't. Don't have the balance for it." He stands up tall on his left leg, and his right foot is an inch off the ground. "You gotta *really* think about the choices you make, kid. You're lucky if you get a second chance."

I run my hand across the spiky hair growing out on my head and shift my eyes toward the floor. "I don't know what I'd do if I couldn't skate . . ."

"It was tough." He shakes his head back and forth. "And for a while I was a complete mess. Started drinkin' and druggin'," he whispers. "I lost everything. My girlfriend, the best girl in the world, left me. And I don't blame her neither. I was a wreck. I'd borrow money. Never pay it back. Show up to work for a day or two. Then disappear for weeks. I was a piece of crap. *A liar.* A cheat and *a liar.* And ya know what I kept tellin' myself? *It was always someone else's fault.* That's what I'd tell myself, pretending it had nothin' to do with me. I burned every bridge I had."

"So then what happened?"

"I woke up. Had to. Woke up one afternoon in an alley. Dried blood caked on my face. Lyin' in a pool of my own piss. And I knew right then, if I didn't do something, I was gonna die. So I got help. Got myself cleaned up. But no one, and I mean *no one* in the entire skateboarding *world* would have *anything* to do with me. Except one person." He motions with his head toward the row of offices in the hallway. "Dirk Davies. He's the only one who gave me a second chance."

I stare at the box cutter lying on the ground. "I lied, Steely. Lied to my parents. Dirk did too. They think I got hurt here."

"Oh." Steely nods staring down at the floor, then looks up at me. "It's tearing you up, huh? Lying to your folks. It's not easy living with lies."

I look at the open door of the board room, shaking my head. "They would sue Dirk if they found out. And I'd be kicked off the team for sure."

"Listen." He walks over and shuts the door. "I'm tellin' you *all* of this for a reason." He leans against a counter. "Dirk's not gonna let go of this mega ramp thing easy. He's working with some fancy helmet company that specializes in high-impact sports. He's developing a special-edition Josh Lowman Mega Helmet that he's gonna market to the world." He shakes his head. "That Dirk. He is something else. I'm tellin' you."

I rub the side of my head. "Why does he want a helmet with my name on it?"

"'Cause he's gonna come to you once you start skating again. He's gonna try and get you back out to Quest's place to skate the mega ramp. And he wants to make sure he has a helmet that'll protect your noggin. That's why." He taps his head with his finger. "And here's what I want you to know. You can choose to do it. You can choose *not* to. But the *choice* is *yours*. No one else's." And then he picks up a box cutter and so do I and we work together in silence until every box is empty and it's time for me to go home.

22

STICKERS

I sit on the bus staring out the window, watching neighborhoods, cars, and people flash by. The bus shudders to a stop at a red light and three kids skateboard past us, charging down the sidewalk together, ollieing over cracks. Nothing fancy, just having fun. When I get off the bus, I check in with my mom, and then walk over to Cody's house. He answers the front door. He sees that it's me and doesn't say a word. "Hey, Cody," I say. "Can I come in?"

"I guess." He opens the door wide enough for me to enter.

"What are you doing?" I ask.

"Homework," he says.

"Mind if I hang out?"

"If you want." He shrugs.

I sit across the table from Cody while he does his geometry. When he's done we go out to the street and I watch him skate. "Hey, Cody," I blurt out as he tailslides along the curb. "I, uh . . . I'm sorry." He keeps skating and I'm not sure if he heard me and I feel kind of stupid, so I say the first thing that pops into my head. "What do you think of a Ford Falcon, the kind Mrs. Thompson drives?"

He stops his skateboard with his foot. "Sweet car," he says, nodding.

"Wanna come to my house for dinner?" I ask.

"Yeah, sure," he says, and that's how I know he heard me.

Later, when we're all sitting around the dinner table, I make my announcement. "Mom, Dad," I say, "I'm gonna buy Mrs. Thompson's car."

Cody's eyes get real big. He glances my way smiling. Both my parents stop eating. "What about Dirk's car?" My mom lays her fork on the table.

"Don't want it. Gonna give it back."

My mom looks at my dad. "Mrs. Thompson's car is old."

"I have ADSK money saved in my bank account," I say. "And no one takes better care of their car than Mrs. Thompson. And I'm sixteen. It's a perfect first car."

My dad runs his index finger back and forth across the stubble on his chin, looks at my mom, and then they both look at me. My mom holds her palms up toward the ceiling. "Okay," they say at the same time, just like that.

As soon as we finish eating dinner, me and Cody walk over to Mrs. Thompson's house and seal the deal. She comes out to the curb with us and watches us peel the FOR SALE signs off the windows. The next day I go to the bank, pay Mrs. Thompson, and she gives me the pink slip. I hold it up to the sun, rays of light filtering through the thin pink paper, my signature and Mrs. Thompson's scrawled along the bottom of the form. I slide it into my back pocket and Mrs. T. hands me the keys to *my very own car*.

After dinner the doorbell rings. I open the door and Cody and Niko stand on the porch with their skateboards dangling at their sides. I hustle upstairs, grab one of my Alpha Dog custom boards, and head back down. "Be back soon," I holler to my parents.

"No skateboarding for you, Josh," my dad shouts back.

Me, Niko, and Cody walk down the street and stop when we get to Mrs. Thompson's place. Niko walks around the entire car, whistles, looks at me and nods. I toss him the keys. "Still can't drive or skate." I point to my head. "You're drivin'."

"Sweet," he says and we pile in. Niko starts the engine. "Where we going?" he asks.

"You know where Big Chad lives?"

Niko nods. "I know where he lives."

"Let's go there first," I say.

We cruise the streets of Green Valley, then pull into Big Chad's driveway. Reaching into the backseat, I grab the skateboard, get out of the car, and walk up to the porch. I lay the board on the doormat, turn around, and hop back into the car. Cody and Niko look at me like I'm crazy. I don't say a word. I just shrug. "Let's get outta here," I say.

We drive over to the back of the Thrifty Save. Cody and Niko air over gaps and stairs, grind along the rails of the loading docks underneath the eerie glow of fluorescent lights while I sit on a pile of wooden pallets and watch. When they're done skating we head to the mini mart for some slushies. Niko gestures toward the parking lot. "You know what your vehicle needs?" Cody and I look at him. "Stickers," he says.

We mob to Cody's house, race into his room, raid his sticker collection, and decorate my car. We plaster stickers on the bumpers, on the doors, and along the back window. When we're done, we stand back and admire our work. "This looks good," Cody says, grinning. "Like a true skater's car."

"It's a *totally* sweet ride." Niko lobs the keys up in the air and catches them.

When we get back to my house, Niko tosses me the keys. "Here you go, Lowman," he says. Cody, crouching down, presses one last sticker onto the back fender. I shove the keys deep into my pocket and look both of them square in the eye. "Thanks," I say, flicking my head toward the car.

"It's cool," Niko says, nodding slowly.

Cody bumps my fist and they both turn around and leave.

"Come skate my half-pipe tomorrow, if you want," I holler after them.

"Sounds good, Lowman," Cody mutters. They shuffle down my driveway, plop their boards on the ground, and push off, the sound of their wheels clicking across grooves in the pavement slowly fading into the night.

23

MAN OF MY WORD

Late Friday afternoon, me and my parents sit in my doctor's office reading worn-out magazines until they finally call my name for my final follow-up exam. A nurse lady dressed in flowery scrubs leads us down a hall. She has me step onto a scale, puts a thermometer under my tongue, takes my blood pressure and listens to my heart, then finally leads us to an examining room where we sit and wait again. Finally my doctor pops into the room.

"Hello, Josh," she says. "Mr. and Mrs. Lowman." She nods her head in their direction and then swivels her head back my way. "How we feeling today?" she asks.

I shrug. "Fine."

"Any headaches, blurred vision, ringing in the ears?"

"Nope." I shake my head.

"Good." She grabs a flashlight-doctor-tool thingy and peers into my eyes. "Look that way." She points toward the door. "Good, now over there." She points in the opposite direction and follows my eyes as they scan across the room.

She sits down on her rolling chair across from me and my parents. "Okay," she says. "I've reviewed your charts and your brain scans. You're a *very* lucky young man. So, as long as there are no symptoms present, you're clear to resume your regular activities. But"—she points her finger at me—"I don't want to see you in here again. You be careful. Understand?"

I look down at my feet and nod. My parents stand up and shake the doctor's hand. When we get home, my mom goes upstairs. My dad pulls a pizza out of the freezer and sets it on the counter. "You're in charge tonight, boss," he says. "You're watching your little brother. Your mom and I are going out."

"Fine by me," I say, reaching for the remote and kicking back on the couch.

"Listen," he says. "What are your plans tomorrow?"

"I was going to drive Dirk's Mustang out to the training facility. Give him back his car. I'll probably hang out with Steely for a while and then take the bus back," I say, surfing through channels.

"The training facility, huh?"

"Yeah, that okay with you?"

"We don't have time for it tonight, but you, your mom, and I need to talk."

I press the MUTE button on the remote and sit up. "What do we need to talk about?"

"Josh." He looks at me, tapping his fingers on the counter. "We don't want you skating."

"Never? You don't want me to skate ever again?"

"I don't know. We need to talk. But in the meantime, no skating out there tomorrow."

I nod slowly, exhaling. "I promise. I won't skate."

My mom comes down the stairs. "Josh, make sure you make Mikey dinner. And don't let him stay up too late." She looks at my dad. "Ready?"

He grabs the car keys from the counter, locking his eyes on mine. "Man of your word?" he asks.

I shift my eyes to the remote in my hand, "Yeah, Dad. Man of my word." He puts his arm around my mom's waist and escorts her to the door.

I drive to the TF first thing in the morning. I'm not sure if Steely's working, but I know a huge shipment of ADSK stuff just came in and I'm stoked when I see a light streaming into the hallway out of the board room door. I go to Dirk's office first. When I walk in, Dirk's reading a bunch of important-looking papers with a pen in his hand. He looks up. "Josh. Good to see you. You gave us quite a scare." He hops out from behind his desk and slides a chair over. "Here, take a seat. How are you feeling?" he asks, studying me.

I dig my hands into my pockets. "Good."

"Sorry I didn't come to the hospital. I just wanted to give you and your family space, you know?"

"Yeah."

"And Taj and Ricky—totally traumatized—they didn't want to go near the hospital. Say they'll *never* skate the mega ramp either." He shakes his head and sighs.

"Here are your keys," I say, laying them on the desk in front of him. "Thanks."

"You don't want the car anymore?"

"Got my own. A Falcon, a Ford Falcon."

"That's an *old* car. Sure you don't want to keep driving the Mustang?" He dangles the keys in front of me.

"Yeah." I nod. "Totally sure."

He raps his knuckles on the desk. "I have something I want to show you." He pops out of his seat. "Follow me," he says, clipping down the hall and turning into the board room, me trailing behind. "Steely, you in here?" he calls out.

"Yeah, right here," Steely hollers from behind a display case. Standing up, he looks at me. "Hey, kid, howya doing?" he asks.

I shrug. "Okay."

Dirk rubs his hands together, walks over to a shelf, and grabs something—a shiny orb that he holds up in one hand. "Do you know what this is?"

I take a closer look. "A helmet?"

"Not just any helmet, a state-of-the-art helmet—what they use in the *NFL*." He turns it over and points to a dial at the back. "This allows you to pump air between two chambers to customize the fit to the rider's head. It's the most advanced technology out there. The safest protection for your cranium that money can buy." He knocks his knuckles against the hollow shell. "See, with this on your head"—he points to me—"you're bulletproof . . . You can skate again, and when you're ready we can get you back up on the mega ramp. I've even worked out a deal with Robby. I'm paying him to let you train out there. The mega ramp is your new training facility if you want it to be."

I dig my hands deeper into my pockets. "I don't know. I mean . . . the mega ramp. It's sketchy, ya know? Super sketchy," I say, shifting from one foot to the other.

Dirk nods in agreement. "Yes, that's true. It is sketchy, but . . ." He takes a deep breath, pausing before he speaks and then clearing his throat. "The mega ramp could be the biggest thing to happen in skateboarding since the urethane wheel. People, lots of people, are finally going to pay attention to skateboarding." He closes his eyes, rubs the sides of his temples, and then holds both of his hands out in front of him with his palms facing up toward the ceiling. "You want to know why?" He looks toward Steely and then back at me, his eyes dancing. "Because it's sketchy. Because people want to watch something where a person has something to lose. Something *has* to be at stake. There has to be *risk* or else it's not worth watching."

"Don't like where you're going with this," Steely grumbles.

Dirk looks at Steely and then back at me. "Okay, let me try this again," he says. He brushes a hand across his head and then waves his index finger in front of him. "Like you say, Josh, the mega ramp *is* sketchy, but that's why it works. Like, uh . . . like, take Roman gladiators for instance. You lose, you die. People want to watch that. *That's* dramatic. Street skating—you don't land a trick, you scrape your elbow, maybe break an ankle, *who cares?* But the mega ramp. Dropping in from eight stories. Riding down a monster. Soaring into the air fifty feet. Don't you see? People. Audiences. *Sponsors* are going to pay attention."

"Yeah, but . . . you lose, you *die*," I say.

He points to the helmet. "But now you don't *have* to. Look, Steely and I watched the footage, you fell for *one reason*—you got speed wobbles because your trucks were loose. It shouldn't have happened. It was avoidable. An accident that happened once and it *never* has to happen again," he says, tapping his index finger on the counter, to the rhythm of his words. He clears his throat again, and then lowers his voice. "When people watch you skate the mega ramp, Josh, they'll *think* you have something to lose, but with your talent and your skill as a skater, and with this helmet on your head, you don't. You see? You're bulletproof, but the people watching don't *know* that. They get their blood sport, their person standing at the top of the ramp risking it all, but we've removed the risk without them knowing it. We're all bulletproof . . . everybody wins."

Steely coughs into his hand, crouches down behind the display case, and starts working again.

Dirk locks his eyes on me. "You remember, Josh. You *know*. You're one of an elite group of skaters who *know* what it feels like to fly down a mega ramp, to soar through the air. That feeling you have afterward. Like you can do *anything* in the world. You *know* what it's like—I saw it in your eyes. And you're good, Josh. *Really* good. You could be the best skater in the world if you keep at it. Why would you walk away from that if you don't have to?"

I pick up the helmet and mess around with the dial, the low sound of hissing air cutting through the silence. I close my eyes, focus on the specks of light wavering in the darkness, and as hard as I try to tell myself I'm done skating mega, I want to see it one more time. As much as I know I should hand Dirk his helmet and keys and walk away forever, I want to feel it one more time. I want to stand at the top of the mega ramp with a pit in my stomach, skin tingling, dropping in, flying, nailing the landing—*one more time*. I open my eyes. Exhale. "Are you *sure* this thing works?" I say, staring at the helmet in my hands.

Dirk nods. "It protects the heads of three-hundred-pound linebackers smacking into each other every day. I think it'll protect yours."

Dirk stands there, trying to read my mind, waiting. "I'll try skating mega again," I say. "On one condition."

"Name it."

"Steely has to be my coach."

Steely rises from behind the glass. Studying my face, he sets a skate deck on the counter.

I look up and meet his gaze. "I want to go to the mega ramp *right* now."

Steely's eyes cut into me. His lips sit tightly across his leathery face. "I don't know why. I just need to see it. I need to go out there. Come with me . . . *Please*," I beg.

Steely sighs.

Dirk claps his hands together. Grabbing the helmet out of my hands, he pats me on the back and motions for us to follow him to his office. Me and Steely stand in the doorway while Dirk talks on the phone. He hangs up, grinning. "Quest's expecting you, but he doesn't have all day." He scoots out from behind his desk. Scooping the helmet into his hands, he flips it over, showing us how to adjust the dials so that it hugs my head perfectly. He's right, it feels bulletproof.

"I can't go with you guys right now. But I trust Steely. Go without me." Dirk hands me the keys to his Mustang and points to the towering stack of documents on his desk. "Grab a new skateboard from the board room. You're all set," he says and then buries his face in a document, twirling a pen in his hand. On the drive out to the mega ramp, my throat feels tight. I'm not sure what to say or how to explain to Steely what's going on in my head because the truth is, even I don't understand it, so we drive to the mega ramp in complete silence. When we get there, Robby's heaving a suitcase into the trunk of his car. He slams the trunk shut and heads our way. "Steely my man, great to see you," he says, shaking our hands. He pats Steely on the back. He swings the gate open and motions for us to enter.

We walk toward the pickup truck that's waiting to take us up the hill. Robby puts a hand on my shoulder. "Dude, I am so sorry about that slam you took . . . It happens, you know? Happens to all of us. It's part of the deal." Dangling the truck keys in front of me, he motions for me to take the driver's seat. "Dirk *begged* me to let you come. Wish I could hang out with you guys but I'm out of town for a couple of weeks. I've got a huge install happening overseas." He leans both of his arms on the side of the pickup. "After the slam you took, it's really important to get you back up there ASAP. Steely'll have to keep an eye on you. And remember"—he points at me—"take it *easy* your first few runs."

I nod.

"And check your trucks, would ya?" Robby turns around and charges toward his house.

Steely places my board on his lap, flips it over, and checks my trucks one more time. He taps his fingers on the dash and fixes his eyes on me. He doesn't say a word, but I know what he's thinking. Gripping the steering wheel, I stare at the mountain in front of me, my heart racing.

"Steely," I say, "I *have* to go up there." I swivel around to face him. "See, I don't *know* if I can drop in again, but I *have* to find out, because if I don't, if I quit right now, I don't know. I just gotta go up there. Does that make any sense?"

Steely sighs. He flicks his fingers toward the mountain, motioning with his hand for me to drive. The truck lurches forward and eventually we arrive at the bottom of the ramp. I park, and we get out. We stand side by side gazing up the slope. I point to the very top platform. "I rolled in from up there a bunch of times."

Steely focuses his eyes directly on me. "I know."

I grab pads and strap them on. Making sure that all my skin is covered, I hop back in the truck, my board and the helmet Dirk gave me resting in the back. "Get in, let's go," I say.

"Nah, I'll watch you from down here." His jaw clenched, he stares at me.

"Please? Come on. I just want you to see it from the top."

Shaking his head back and forth, he walks over and slides into the passenger seat. I put the pickup in gear and we drive up the mountainside. We pass the first platform, then the second. When we get to the highest platform I park the truck and hop out. Steely follows me, rocking back and forth up the stairs. The sun is directly over us, bearing down on the valley below; in the distance a strip of blue ocean stretches across the horizon.

I climb onto the platform and peer down the edge with my new helmet fastened under my chin. I sit down, set the board next to me, hold my knees to my chest, and I feel like I'm on top of the world. Closing my eyes, I think about flying down the face, floating through the air, the force of gravity pulling me back down where I belong, and I remember what it feels like in my flesh and bones to be soaring, and even though I *know* I'm man enough to drop in . . . I'm not sure I'm man enough to choose not to.

I stand up, set my board on the edge, and hold it in place with my foot. I look down the steep slope, ready to drop in. Scanning the horizon, I spot my town, Green Valley. I think about my friends—Erin, Cody, Niko, and Brendon too. I stare at the vertical wall of the quarter-pipe in the distance, and then I glance over at Steely. Motionless, his face is tilted toward the sky. I wish he'd say something, but he stands silent and I know that whatever I do, I'm in this on my own. I roll my board back and forth with one foot, my heart practically busting a hole through my chest, my head swirling, *knowing* I can make the drop, *knowing* I can pull the landing. But then I think about my mom and dad, and like phantoms, their faces hang over me, their voices whisper in my ear—*man of your word, be a man of your word*, and Steely, holding vigil through it all, leans against the rail, the rhythm of his breathing the only sound he makes.

Swallowing hard, I'm practically bawling. I glance down at my board, close my eyes . . . and then I push my board over the edge— feel myself fly, wind against my face, me, on a skateboard, soaring . . . floating above it all. And when I open my eyes, I watch the board ghost-ride down the slope without me, gain speed, bounce and clank along the surface without a rider, until it careens off the ramp and disappears, a cloud of dust rising from the earth where it lands. I hop off the platform and look at Steely. "Let's get out of here," I say. He looks at me, nodding, and finally he speaks. "*Good man*," he says, pointing a thick finger directly at the center of my chest.

24

ALL EXCEPT ONE

Driving back to the training facility, I stare out of the front window. Steely's at the wheel and we drive in silence. When we get to the TF, Steely walks toward the board room and gestures with his head for me to follow.

"Steely," I say, "I'm not coming with you." I hold up the keys and helmet. "I'm returning these. Giving them back to Dirk . . . for good. I'm done. I'm quitting ADSK."

He buries both hands deep into his pockets and nods slowly. "Oh," he says, "okay." He turns to leave, then turns back to face me, his shoulders back, his barrel chest sticking out in front of him like a lieutenant in the army. "Listen," he says. "You stop by and see me every once in a while. You hear?"

We lock eyes. "I will, Steely. Thanks," I say. "For everything."

He reaches out and shakes my hand. "You're a good man, Josh. You hear, me? A good man, and a hell of a skater. Don't you ever forget that." He turns on his heels, marches away, and I watch him walk down the hallway, turn into the board room, and disappear.

I take a deep breath and head into Dirk's office. He looks up from the papers he's working on when he hears me enter. "So how'd it go?" he asks, studying my face.

"I didn't do it. Didn't drop in," I say.

"Oh. Well, we can get you out there again tomorrow. Robby gave me the thumbs-up for you to skate at his place while he's out of town."

I stare at my shoes for a second and then look Dirk in the eyes. "The things is, I'm done skating mega."

He tilts his head. "What do you mean?"

"I'm done skating mega and I'm done skating for the ADSK team."

Leaning forward in his chair, he places both elbows on the desk in front of him. "Look," he says. "You took a bad fall. It happens. You probably just need a little more time. But quitting? Come on. You have a bright future. Whatever's going on with you, we'll work it out."

I shake my head. "There's nothing to work out. Thank you for giving me the opportunity to skate for your team. See if Jagger Michaels wants these," I say and place the special-edition mega helmet and the keys to his car on his desk. "He'll fit right in with the Alpha team."

Dirk stands up, sputtering on his words, "Alpha dominance," "nothing to lose," something about a contract . . . and I turn around and leave.

When I finally get home, my mom and dad sit on the back patio eating a late lunch. I pull up a chair. Swallowing hard, I stare at my hands folded in my lap and before my parents tell me I have to quit skating for good, I start talking.. I tell them that I was in the hospital because I hurt myself on the mega ramp, *not* on the vert ramp at the ADSK training facility, that I hid it from them, and that I'm sorry. *Really* sorry. They're quiet for a while and then my dad stands up and starts pacing back and forth across the patio. My mom and I watch him walk and then he stops and comes over and sits back down. He leans across the table and I have a hard time looking him in the eye. "You mean to tell me you were riding some kind of giant ramp without our permission after almost dying from a brain injury, *and* you got hurt out there? *And then* you lied to us?" He talks slowly, enunciating each word.

I cradle my forehead in the palm of my hand. "I know. It's bad. Really bad."

"And what about Dirk? He had to know. He's in on this." My dad slaps the table and leans back in his chair. "We're going to destroy him."

"No, Dad. Please don't. It's not Dirk's fault. It's mine. I take full responsibility. What I did was wrong. I know it and I'm sorry. But don't pin this on anyone else but me."

My mom purses her lips, and I can see tears welling up in the corners of her eyes.

I let go of a deep breath, stand up, and then sit back down. "Look," I say, "I know you have no reason to believe me right now, but you have to believe me when I say that you don't have to worry about me skating the mega ramp or trying some crazy trick to win a skate competition ever again because I quit ADSK. For good. I'm happy riding at the Green Valley Skatepark, and right here in our backyard with Niko and Cody. So, please-don't make me stop skating. I promise you, I've learned my lesson."

For the first time in a long time, every word that I say to my parents is true—100 percent true—and I'm not sure what they're going to do to me, if they're going to put me on restriction for the rest of my life or take Dirk Davies to court, but the truth is I don't care. It feels so good to tell the truth, to have things out in the open, and for the first time in a long time I look at both of my parents in their eyes. They stare back at me and for some reason, I think about Brendon, sitting next to my hospital bed, setting down a bag of rocks. Sitting across from my parents, I think I've set down my rocks too. All except one.

"Mom . . . Dad," I say, "I know I'm gonna be on restriction for a while. I'll take whatever punishment you dish out, but do you think I can have a few hours this afternoon to take care of something?"

"What do you need to take care of?" my dad asks, slowly tapping his fingers on the table.

"I need to see Erin. I need to make things right with her, that's all."

My mom reaches across the table. Placing her hand on top of my father's, she looks into his face and then into mine. "He's taking responsibility for his actions. Let him go," she whispers.

My father sighs. He looks across the backyard and squeezes my mom's hand, slowly nodding. I walk over to their side of the table, bend over, hug them both, and then I go to my room. I throw on my old clothes and look in the mirror. My hair's growing out spiky, so I throw an old ball cap on too. I grab the keys to my car, bolt down the stairs, and drive over to Erin's house.

"You busy?" I ask when she answers the door.

"Not really," she says.

"Then come with me." I hold out my hand. I clear my throat. "I, uh . . . I want to take you on a date."

"A date?" She stares back at me.

"Yeah. Like, not just hanging out. I'm asking you out. Like on an official date," I say, looking into her green eyes. "Let's go for a ride in my car." I motion with my head toward the driveway.

She doesn't take her eyes off mine. "A date . . . okay." She pops back into the house, grabs her things, and walks out the door. "Let's go," she says.

I loop my arm through hers, walk her to my old car covered in skate stickers, open her door, and then slam it shut behind her. I hop in the driver's seat and turn the key.

"Where we going?" she says.

"You'll see." I smile.

We drive through the valley heading west for a while. With the windows rolled down, a warm breeze brushes against our skin. Erin's hair whips around her face. She looks over at me every once in a while and smiles. The sun sinks lower and lower in the distance. When we finally come to a lookout spot over the ocean, I park the car. Waves slowly roll to shore, and a line of pelicans glides along the surface of the water. We sit there for a while taking it all in. I think about Dirk Davies and ADSK. I think about my mom and dad and Steely and choices. And when I look over and see Erin Campbell sitting next to me in the front seat of my car, I think about what matters the most.

"Erin," I say. "No matter what, I want to be your friend forever."

She turns in her seat to face me. "Even when we're old?"

"Even when we're old," I say.

She shakes her head. "Josh." I reach across the front seat and so does she. We sit in my car, holding hands, staring straight ahead into the limitless future. Me and Erin, together, focused on a wavering orange ball dancing on the horizon, we watch the sun slide slowly through the sky and melt into the sea.